THE TIGRAN NOVELLAS: 2176

M. W. DENDLER

BY M. W. DENDLER

At the Corner of Magnetic and Main

The Tigran Chronicles: The Gathering

The Tigran Novellas: 2176

The Tigran Chronicles: The Rescues

FOR YOUNG READERS

Bianca: The Brave Frail and Delicate Princess

Bianca: Journey to Ryuugito

Poppy and Marigold

Cats in the Mirror Series

Book 1: *Why Kimba Saved The World*

Book 2: *Vacation Hiro*

Book 3: *Miss Fatty Cat's Revenge*

Book 4: *Slinky Steps Out*

Book 5: *Kimba's Christmas*

Book 6: *Snickerdoodle's Shenanigans*

And the Companion Books

Max's Wild Night

Dottie's Daring Day

Published by Serenity Mountain Publishing

Midland, Michigan

The Tigran Novellas: 2176

©2025 by Meg Welch Dendler

All rights reserved.

www.megdendler.com

First Edition

ISBN: 979-8990827745

Cover design by Sweet N' Spicy Designs.

Interior design by Serenity Mountain Publishing.

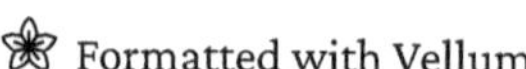 Formatted with Vellum

CONTENTS

These novellas take place in the year before the epilogue of *The Tigran Chronicles: The Gathering*. They are not meant to stand apart from that book, so be sure you've read it first.

Recovering Reynaldo

CHAPTER 1

JUNE 1, 2176

General Carl Thompson loaded two laser pistols into his holsters, along with several backup chargers. His entire future depended on the success of this mission.

Reynaldo was going to be set free. Today. One way or another.

For a year after Reynaldo, Taliya, and the four pterodragons were kidnapped from the refugee camp outside Winnipeg, there had been no sign of the black panthran. Carl was able to rescue Taliya within a few days, which was vital because she was not of financial value. Her only use had been as ransom for her unique, highly sought-after kits. The kidnappers would have killed her if given much more time.

The dragons were important assets in their own right. They were genetic experiments that should not be in the wrong hands, and both the U.S. and Canadian governments wanted them back. Rumor was the animals had been stealthily taken away from the North American continent. Frankly, Carl wasn't terribly concerned about the dragons. They were valuable and would be cared for, wherever they were.

All he could focus on was Reynaldo.

Nightly, Carl woke from nightmares of his mate being abused. Finding him, but not being able to save him. Seeing the panthran in the distance, but unable to run, feeling like his feet were stuck in mud. Waking with a shout, covered in sweat. Rey had been through so much horror in his life. That he could be suffering right at that moment consumed Carl's thoughts.

Finally, after that year of fruitless searching, the ex-girlfriend of the man who held Reynaldo called the government hotline with a tip on where to find the panthran. Not because she cared about the creature. Just to screw over her ex.

That was fourteen months and five days ago.

At first, the new laws on keeping genetic creations captive and "owning" them were not fully established and passed through Congress. Once they were, lawyers and local police began negotiations with the man and his buddies, who lived on a well-armed compound in Mississippi and refused to release Reynaldo—completely unimpressed with laws of any kind from the new government.

It was a high-profile case due to the connection with the refugee camp, but the captors would not yield or even discuss releasing their prisoner. After simply refusing to acknowledge the new laws, they insisted on being "grand-fathered" in. No amount of persuasion would shift them or even allow law enforcement onto the property to check the panthran's condition. Every attempt was met with military-level resistance.

Samson the ligran—now part of the government legal team—and the FBI took over the case, with the same results. Samson had to concede: the peaceful, legal solution was not going to work.

If Reynaldo was going to walk free, it was going to be by force.

Carl had been ready to attack that very day. Had been ready to carry out a rescue from the moment Rey was found. But he was bound by the rules and regulations of the U.S. Army he served. His desperate fear that the kidnappers would kill Reynaldo to eliminate the problem haunted every hour. He tried to organize mercenaries, but his superiors got wind of the plan and threatened to lock him in the brig. In prison, Carl knew he'd be useless, so he fumed and made sure no one forgot about Reynaldo's plight.

The career military man had never expected to find himself in love with one of the genetic creations he risked his life to save from corrupt government scientists and the mechanisms of then-President Kerkaw. He hadn't been interested in a relationship with anyone at all. There was too much to accomplish. Too much moving around and high-stakes military action. Ultimately, any honest relationship at that time would definitely end him up in the brig, if not dead.

But the moment his eyes met Reynaldo's in that miserable cesspool of a government lab, Carl knew he was in trouble. Highly illegal, punishable by death trouble. Either for a same-sex partner or one of a different species.

Carl's earliest missions for the rebel army had been to rescue genetic creations from secret government labs. Then *Major* Carl Thompson was technically an Enforcer, part of the U.S. Army. But he'd grown more and more disillusioned by new government policies. Even before the Gathering, Carl had been recruited by the rebel forces to act as a mole within Kerkaw's Army.

But then the Gathering began in the fall of 2172, and those questionable policies became violent actions nearing genocide. The public executions and imprisonments focused on tigran. Most of the world was not even aware of the wide variety of human/animal hybrids that different governments were experimenting with. Unlike the tigran, who lived among humans, Reynaldo was created in a lab and raised there by scientists who were more interested in studying him than caring for him, and their main goal was to produce more panthran, especially black ones.

Every worker in a facility signed lengthy disclosure statements, though rumors often snuck out. Through his connections on both sides of the war, Carl heard more than rumors. Working undercover for the rebels, he'd been active in seven facility rescues so far. The day he'd helped coordinate the raid on the panthran lab in October of 2172 was no different.

Except that was the day Carl met Reynaldo.

Six of them—four rebel soldiers and two drivers—had assembled in the dark hours of night to break into the lab and free whoever was being held there, then destroy the lab and all of the research. Any creatures rescued would be transported to the safety of a refugee camp in Canada.

The facility lay in a valley surrounded by hills and forest. Soldiers had been observing it and reporting. Carl was fairly sure they knew all the security measures to avoid and disarm, but nerves still churned his stomach. It would be days before he could consider every creature safe and his cover not blown. If he was ever caught during one of these rescue missions, Carl knew he'd be shot on the spot. Enforcers had a great disdain for trials and legal complications.

As far as the U.S. military was concerned, he was on vacation. In Hawaii. Doctored photos were being posted on his media pages, depicting him enjoying the beach surrounded by pretty women in skimpy bathing suits. It was a cover story for more than just his involvement with the rebels. Better to be considered a "player" than a man who was indifferent to cleavage.

Sergeant Dan—also undercover from Kerkaw's Army —crouched next to him behind a row of bushes, using heat-and-radar-sensing binoculars to scan the facility. He and Dan had been a team through five other rescues, but even the familiar, trusted presence didn't calm Carl's anxiety that night. An owl hooted in the woods behind them, startling him. He breathed in and out slowly, trying to settle his nerves.

"Only seeing ten bodies in there," Dan said, frowning. "We've heard double that number."

"Maybe they're too deep inside for us to register from here," Carl suggested. "Or underground. Some metals and concrete block the sensors."

"Could be. We'll find out soon enough."

A small blue light on Carl's communicator flashed three times. That was the signal. Dan glanced at the light, patted Carl on the shoulder, and then led the way toward the building. Staying low, they moved slowly, ready for any unanticipated alarm or security. Carl spotted the other two soldiers coming down a hill across from them. When they all reached the back door, Dan used a forged access card to unlock the building.

Inside, the industrial-style halls were dark, with only the faint red glow of the exit signs radiating off the white concrete walls and floor. Carl and Dan's mission was to head to the basement, check for anything alive, and destroy any research or computer they could find. The other team would take care of the ten creatures on the main floor and destroy records upstairs once they knew the captives were out. With a nod, the teams split up to accomplish their objectives.

Slowly opening the heavy metal door to the stairwell, Dan led the way through. The two men crept down the steps, guns drawn and ready. At the entrance to the basement, they paused. It wasn't clear from the intel if there would be a guard on duty. So far in these raids, they hadn't needed to shoot anyone.

They'd kill you without flinching, he reminded himself.

As planned, Dan stepped back and let Carl take the lead. He opened the door a crack. No alarm sounded. Pushing it a bit wider, the smell of the lab hit him. Stale, moldy air and sewage, wrapped up with other nauseating odors. Anger swelled in his chest, knowing there might be creatures with highly sensitive noses forced to live surrounded by that stench. Did the scientists have no pride in their creations?

In one swift motion, Carl pushed the door open and Dan stepped through, gun at the ready. But there was nothing. Maybe, because of the secret nature of their experiments, security was light. Who would even know about this place to try to break in?

Dan flipped on the light at the top of his pistol, scanned the room, and revealed several cells, though Carl couldn't see anyone inside. He turned on his gun-mounted torch as well.

"Hello?" a deep voice called out hesitantly from the direction of the cells.

"Where are the keys?" Dan asked.

"In the desk over in the corner," the voice said. "Second drawer on the right."

While Dan searched, Carl headed down the row of rudimentary cages. It was like some horror movie zoo or prison—cruelty and neglect that only existed hundreds of years ago. Thick iron bars with metal sleeping platforms hanging on the sides. Bare concrete floors. A metal toilet and small sink in each cell, but no showers. The first few cages held the shapes of sleeping creatures, but in the fourth cage, Carl was met with the glow of haunting amber eyes.

"We're going to get you out of here," Carl said. "Transports are waiting to take you to Canada."

The creature blinked twice. "Canada?"

"There's a camp there. They'll keep you safe and give you a good, normal life."

"What kind of normal life is there out in the world for monsters like us?"

"I don't risk my life to rescue *monsters*," Carl said firmly. "Only living beings. Part-human beings, who deserve to live in freedom."

The male rose and moved to stand at the bars of the cage, eye to eye with Carl—well over six feet tall. The captive was covered in jet-black fur—the reason he'd been hard to distinguish in the darkness. His ears were more pointed, nose and jaw wider and more jaguar-like, but in general built like a tigran. Like Bagheera from that old movie had decided to walk upright. Carl found himself mesmerized by the deep-golden eyes, full of sadness. He almost reached through the bars to touch him, to comfort him.

"See. Monster."

"No," Carl said with a firm shake of his head. "Genetic creation. Panthran?"

"That's what they call us."

Dan headed their way with the key card but hesitated at the sight of the massive male standing right at the bars of the cell door. No creature had ever been violent or dangerous during a rescue, but there was always a first time.

"I'm Carl, and this is Dan. We're soldiers with the rebel army. What's your name?"

"Reynaldo. What rebel army?"

Carl and Dan exchanged looks. It was highly possible the creatures in this basement prison knew nothing about the Gathering, Kerkaw, or the war. They would only have the information their captors provided.

"Don't worry about that now, Reynaldo," Dan said. "We need to get you out of here before someone shows up to stop us."

The other prisoners were stirring at the sound of voices.

"Friends," Carl said, "we're not going to hurt you. We're here to set you free. There's a safe camp waiting for you, where you will have a home and food and whatever else you need. Please trust us. Soldiers are waiting until you're outside to destroy this lab so no other creatures can be trapped and treated like experiments."

"But we *are* experiments," a female voice said.

"Not to us." Dan headed her way.

He swiped the key over one lock after another, opening the seven cells. The occupants stepped out slowly. They were all panthran, some with patchy and matted fur. All completely naked and hunched with hopelessness. One female clutched two kits at her side. While she was black, they were tawny and spotted, like a leopard. As he did a quick head count, Carl wondered if the ten creatures upstairs were panthran or something else.

"Twenty-five?" Dan said.

Carl nodded in agreement.

Reynaldo limped out into the light from their torches. There were slash marks on his arms where fur was missing—and Carl suspected on his back as well—from being recently whipped. Even a human nose could smell the blood. Rage burned Carl's throat.

"There's nothing down here to destroy," Dan said, shining his light around the basement. "Just the cells. All the research must be upstairs."

"Opening the door or the cages may have set off a silent alarm," Carl said. "Let's get outta here."

Dan headed toward the exit, and the panthran started to follow him, though a couple held back.

"It'll be okay," Carl assured them. "But we have to hurry."

Maybe they were used to obeying humans' orders—especially ones with guns—but the whole group was soon up the stairs and heading out of the building. Carl could see the kits were terrified, the whites around their eyes flashing in the darkness. Reynaldo and a few others were struggling—injured or sick. As Reynaldo staggered and lagged behind the group, Carl moved to his side.

"Let me help."

He could tell Reynaldo wanted to refuse, but the panthran cautiously wrapped an arm around Carl's shoulder. The soldier put an arm around his waist, carrying part of his weight. Like an old-fashioned three-legged race, they hurried away from the building.

"Up here," Dan whisper-called, motioning toward the hill he and Carl had come down earlier.

A chirp of birdsong came from his right, and Carl spotted ten creatures from the main level of the lab running toward them. One looked like a cheetah/human mix and had five kits with him. A rebel soldier followed behind with her gun raised, alert for an attack from the woods.

As the group climbed, Carl looked back and noticed a red light blipping on the top of the building. Adrenaline flashed through his body. He pulled out his communicator with his free hand and pressed the alert button, warning the soldier still inside to get out. Rescuing the creatures and escaping to safety was the main objective. Destroying research wasn't worth risking that.

"We need to move!" he shouted to the group. "Go!"

They sped up, and Carl suspected the panthran could smell the anxiousness from him. It was unnerving to be surrounded by creatures who knew what you were thinking and feeling simply from your odor. Reynaldo gripped his arm around Carl's shoulders and hurried his pace, but Carl could tell from his breathing that the creature was struggling and in pain.

"Almost there."

Reynaldo gasped. "I can do it."

As the group reached the top of the hill, they waited for the last stragglers and the kits. Looking up at them, Carl noticed an orange light reflecting off the black fur. After he and Reynaldo stumbled to the top, he turned back and sighed in appreciation at the multiple fires shining from windows throughout the building. *Burn it all down.*

"I'm clear," a voice came through his communicator, "but scans show three vehicles incoming. Load up now!"

Carl didn't need to repeat the order. The panthran looked panicked, but he motioned toward the waiting transports, hidden in some trees nearby. Everyone ran and piled inside—Carl and Dan's charges into one, while the other group stuck together in the second vehicle.

"Paxton?" one of the panthran females called out. "Wait!"

Carl carefully deposited Reynaldo in a seat and turned to her. "What's wrong?"

"My kit," she said, starting to leave the transport. "He was right behind me."

Carl grabbed her arm and helped her out of the vehicle, worried the kit might not trust him. They ran back, the female scenting the air. She froze at the sound of a whimper, turned to the side, and ran that direction.

The kit was on the ground and struggling to free his legs from a thick weed. Maybe too scared to call for help. Carl pulled out his KA-BAR knife to cut the vines free, and Paxton's mother scooped him into her arms.

As they ran back to the transport, floodlights lit up the

property, including their path to safety. The rhythmic *whop, whop, whop* of a helicopter sounded in the distance.

"Go!" Carl yelled.

The female and her kit raced across the field and leaped into the transport. Carl couldn't see anyone following them—no sign of the vehicles the second team had spotted—but he knew it wouldn't be long. After one last scan of the area, Carl climbed into the truck.

Dan closed the door behind him. "I did a count. Everyone's here now."

The *schwep* of laser fire sounded in the woods, and three shots pinged off the roof of the truck. Dan banged on the wall twice to signal the drivers. The transport lifted and sped away, throwing Carl into the seat next to Reynaldo, who was now wrapped in a green Army blanket. Carl leaned his head back on the wall and tried to catch his breath. The rank smell in the hold was overwhelming—fear mixed with unwashed fur and body odors. It was tempting to grab a mask and filter, but he didn't want to offend their passengers, who were surely more than aware of the stench.

Next to him, Reynaldo slumped in his seat. Carl leaned over to say something encouraging and realized the creature was unconscious.

"Shit!"

Shifting to the floor, Carl pulled the panthran over onto his side. Even in the dim light of the transport, he could see that blood had soaked through the blanket in spots. Lifting it out of the way, he discovered a dozen long cuts across Reynaldo's back, blood oozing through the fur. Wounds only a day or two old. No smell of infection, yet. There was blood on the sleeve and side of Carl's uniform as well from the escape. He managed to do some physical checks, monitoring the panthran's breathing and heart rate—basic triage skills he'd learned in training. Then he wrapped the blanket around Reynaldo again and sighed, not sure what else to do for the moment.

"You got here just in time," one of the males sitting across from them said. "They were done with him."

"Done?"

"He refused to breed, which is our whole purpose."

"That's why they whipped him?"

"I think this time was more about Rey asking to work with the horses again."

An image of something centaur-like, an actual horse/human mix, flashed through Carl's mind. "What horses?"

"At the government stables. Since he wouldn't breed with the females, they thought he was defective. Sent him to shovel crap and keep the stalls clean. But the horses really took to him. I heard the guards say he was the best trainer the military ever had. He'd worked there for a few years before they brought him home to avoid getting caught up in the Gathering."

"They whipped him because he wanted to go back?"

"Maybe. I guess. Our new guards were Enforcers, not scientists. Didn't need a reason. Reynaldo always stood up for us. The guards didn't appreciate that. They decided to show him how difficult animals should be treated. Then they locked him up alone so none of us could help. Did it again yesterday."

Carl turned back to Reynaldo and double-checked his heart rate and breathing. Both were slow but steady.

"If he didn't die on his own, they'd have killed him soon enough," the male added, pulling his own blanket closer around his shoulders.

Carl sat on the transport floor and rested one hand on Reynaldo's shoulder. "Then I'm glad we made it in time." *What a waste. Why would anyone want to murder such an amazing creature?*

They all sat in silence for the next hour while the transport whooshed along, occasionally changing directions with a sudden jerk. The windows were blackened, so Carl had no idea if they were being followed or where they were. The driver in the cockpit had her orders. She would stop as soon as it was safe. Beyond Reynaldo, there were definitely some medical needs on board, and they all looked like they could use a meal.

Finally, the transport slowed and came to a halt. Carl's heart raced, worried they'd been caught, until the driver banged twice, opened the back door, and smiled in at the group.

"We got away cleanly. We'll take a break here at this small military camp," she said. "Don't wander far. Come 'round to the front of the transport if you're hungry, and let one of the soldiers know if you're injured."

Once she stepped back, the panthran climbed out of

the vehicle and headed straight for the front—hunger beating out all other needs. Reynaldo didn't move, and Carl laid his hand across the panthran's forehead, not sure how to tell if there was a fever. He seemed warm, but that could be how the creatures always felt.

"What's going on there?" the driver asked.

"He's in rough shape. Exhausted and has probably lost a lot of blood. They'd been whipping him. Get a medic."

"Yes, sir."

The driver jogged off, leaving Carl alone in the back of the transport with the still-unconscious Reynaldo.

"You can rest now," Carl mumbled. "I won't let anything happen to you."

They were comforting words to share with a rescued prisoner, but he found he genuinely meant it. Whatever happened to the rest of the group, Carl felt tethered to seeing Reynaldo safely delivered to the refugee camp.

The panthran opened his eyes, and Carl watched as his pupils expanded and dilated, probably trying to figure out where he was. The panthran tensed and started to sit up.

"No," Carl said quietly, "give it a second. We're stopped for a break. It's safe. Everyone is safe."

The golden eyes regarded him, and Reynaldo relaxed.

"Is everyone here? All of them?"

"We have twenty-five of your group," Carl said. "And ten creatures from the lab upstairs. That's all we could find at the facility."

"Yes, that's all of us." He sighed. "Are there any injuries? I don't remember much once we started running."

"No one was hurt in the escape. A doctor is on the way to help you."

"I'll be fine," Reynaldo said. "I've been worse."

Fury stormed in Carl's chest. *What kind of demented men felt the need to beat this creature nearly to death?* Even if that wasn't their actual goal, they clearly didn't mind if that was the end result.

Reynaldo sat up carefully, and Carl didn't stop him this time. He wasn't sure how to help, though. During the escape was one thing, but he didn't want to risk being condescending or hurting the male's pride. Reynaldo winced, showing his white fangs, and wrapped one arm around his middle.

"Ribs?" Carl asked, having had broken or cracked ones a few times in his life.

"Yeah. The guards love punches and kicks to the ribcage. Little effort, big effect."

A young woman in a medic uniform peeked into the back of the transport, her eyes wide and scared-looking. "Heard you need some assistance back here."

Carl motioned her in, and she tentatively climbed inside with a medical bag. It seemed like she was frightened of the black panthran—possibly the first mixed-species creature she'd ever treated—but she'd have to get over that quickly.

"Hey, there," she said, standing just out of reach. "I'm Francie. Do you mind if I take a look at your injuries? We should get you some antibiotics so you can start healing on the trip."

Carl headed off any attempt to dissuade her. "This is Reynaldo, and he's going to tell you he's fine. To go look after the others. But he's not, and there are more doctors who can see to the rest of the group."

Francie and Reynaldo both stared at him, then Reynaldo laughed for a moment before grabbing his ribs in pain.

"He's right," Reynaldo admitted with a gasp. "I was going to say that. And yes, you can check my wounds."

Carl hauled himself up onto the seat next to the panthran, and Francie sat down on the other side as Reynaldo lowered the blanket. She paused with one hand in the air at the sight of his back.

"Holy shit," she said. "You need stitches. A *lot* of stitches." She seemed to consider what she had in her bag, picked up a small roll of bandaging—comically useless— and frowned. "Let's start some antibiotics and get you to the medical tent for cleanup. It would be better to wait on stitches until you're at the Winnipeg camp. We don't have time now, and you should *not* be conscious for that."

Reynaldo shrugged. "It'll heal. Always has before."

Francie huffed and dug around in her bag. "What kind of monsters were you living with?"

"I thought *we* were the monsters," Reynaldo said.

"I told you, I don't risk my life to save monsters," Carl said firmly. "You are a genetic creation, one of thousands. And none of you are monsters."

Looking into Reynaldo's eyes, Carl really wanted to say that he was the most incredible male of any species ever but didn't want to spook him. They still had a long way to travel, and Carl needed the panthran to trust him, not be leery of him.

Francie gave Reynaldo a shot of antibiotics, then sighed. "I wish we could do more now. Once you get some food, let's see about bandaging and pain killers."

Three little panthran faces, all tawny and spotted, peeked up over the edge of the transport opening.

"Rey-Rey, are you okay?" one asked.

"I'll be fine, Pax. Just like always. Did you get something to eat?"

"Yes, sir. Can I bring you something? You must be starving."

Carl already suspected Reynaldo would say he was fine, so he headed him off again. "We'll be right there. Why don't you pick out some of the best bits for him and serve up a plate."

The kit seemed pleased with that answer and scampered off on a mission with the other two in tow.

"When was the last time you ate?" Carl asked.

"I'm not sure."

Carl stood up. "Time for some food, then. As God is my witness, you'll never go hungry again."

Francie chuckled, but Reynaldo only tipped his head.

"It's from an old movie," Carl said with a smile. "About another war in America. I'll pull it up for you once you're safe in Canada."

"Canada. That sounds so far away. Another country."

"It's not too bad, and you can sleep while we travel. Best to get you all there as quickly as possible, just in case."

"In case the Enforcers catch us." Reynaldo stood up slowly.

Carl grimaced and tried not to think about that. He climbed out of the transport and then helped Reynaldo down. Once his feet were on the ground, the panthran turned with determination, grasping Carl's arms and facing him squarely.

"If they do . . . If we're caught, don't let them take us alive. Not me. Not the females. Not the kits. None of us."

Carl felt his knees go weak from the intensity of the contact, as well as the seriousness of the unexpected demand.

"I know you think you'd just rescue us again," Reynaldo said, his golden eyes staring into Carl's dark ones, "and maybe you could. But the punishments they would hand out before then . . . I can't watch the kits be tortured, starved, and beaten."

Carl nodded, but those last words hit like a stab deep in his gut. He didn't get the impression the panthran was prone to exaggeration or drama. If Reynaldo believed that would happen, it must be because it already had, at least to some extent. To the kits.

"Promise me," Reynaldo said, squeezing Carl's arms. "If all hope is lost, and the Enforcers have us, kill everyone. Blow it all up. Don't let them take us back."

Carl swallowed—understanding, wanting to agree, but he just couldn't. "Let's get moving so it never comes to that."

Reynaldo let go of his arms with a frustrated sigh. They headed to the front of the transport, and Reynaldo accepted the plate of food Paxton had devotedly prepared for him.

"Eat all of that," Carl said, "and then head to the medical tent. Paxton, you make sure he goes there, okay? I'm putting you in charge of him."

The kit nodded soberly and glanced up at Reynaldo. Carl didn't wait to see the response, suspecting the panthran would comply just to keep Paxton happy. It gave the soldier a chance to put some distance between himself and the horrific demand Reynaldo had made. Carl grabbed a handful of jerky from a tray and looked for the officer in charge. He found her going over maps with Dan, two other soldiers, and the new drivers.

"Thompson," she said with a glance of acknowledgment. "You get the injured panthran seen to?"

"Yes, Colonel," he said, saluting and then sitting down with the group. "I know it's not routine procedure, but maybe we can give him a sedative for the trip?"

"Speak to medical about it," she said to a private, who rushed off with the message.

Carl chewed on his jerky as the officer showed the fresh drivers what routes to take, getting it all pro-grammed into their coms. They'd be back on the road shortly. The area around them was quiet. Most of the troops were asleep. While it was probably best to avoid scaring the rescued creatures with too many humans—and the inevitable gawking—he hoped there were thousands of troops on hand who were ready to take the fight for freedom straight to Kerkaw.

Once the colonel was done with directions, she spoke into her communicator, something about how to handle the next part of the trip. They were shifting into long-haul transports with simple bathroom facilities, so the group would not be stopping again. The refugee camp was roughly twenty hours away—if everything went smoothly.

"Thompson," she said, pointing her communicator his direction, "medical wants to speak with you about the injured panthran you're in charge of."

"I am?"

"According to *him* you are. Go see to it. Almost time to load up."

Carl stood, quickly saluted, and jogged to the tent. He spotted Reynaldo sitting on a raised cot with a clean sheet wrapped around his waist while a medic fussed with his back. He wondered if the panthran was uncomfortable with his lack of clothing now that he was out in the world or if the medic had covered him up. Reynaldo spotted Carl and raised one hand slightly in greeting. Under the bright lights, Carl realized the panthran had clear rosette markings under his black fur—more like a jaguar than a leopard or panther. Panthran was clearly a very generic name.

"You Thompson?" the medic asked.

"Yeah. How's my friend here?"

"Torn up, man. Seriously torn up."

Reynaldo tried to laugh but clutched his ribs.

"Colonel says you want him sedated for the trip," the medic said. "But our furry dude here refuses."

Reynaldo's eyes went wide, and he shook his head. "No. Not a chance."

"It's going to be a long time in that transport," Carl said. "There's a spot where you can lie down, but a mild sedative would help you sleep part of that time at least."

"But what if we're attacked or something goes wrong? No. I need to be clear-headed. It's just pain. I can take it."

The medic shrugged one shoulder. "You make the call," he said to Carl.

Reynaldo's eyes bored into his, and Carl caught his breath at the intensity of the stare. It seemed like this was the alpha male of the panthran group. The one who defended them from their jailers. Carl tried to put himself in the creature's position. No matter how injured he was, he would want to stay alert until he knew his troops were safe. Was it really any less important, what Reynaldo wanted? The sedative wasn't going to help heal him, only make him more comfortable.

"Whatever you want to do," he said, and Reynaldo looked relieved.

"I've cleaned him up a bit and given him some pain killers, but we don't have time to stitch all of this now," the medic said. "Transports are loading in ten minutes."

"Don't worry about it." Reynaldo shrugged. "It'll heal on its own eventually."

The medic exchanged a look with Carl, and he shrugged in return.

"Let's get you ready to go then," Carl said.

The medic placed a large white pad across the worst of the bloody slash marks on Reynaldo's back, then wrapped it in place. The panthran flinched as the gauze strips crossed his chest.

"What about the ribs?" Carl said.

Reynaldo frowned. "Never mind."

The medic looked confused. "What about his ribs?"

"There's nothing to be done about it right now," Reynaldo said. "Let's go."

He stood up, pausing for a second when some pain must have hit, and headed out of the medical tent, back toward his group. The kits ran to him, and Carl wondered if any of them were his. None of the females seemed particularly attached to him, but that didn't mean he wasn't the father of their kits. Then he remembered the comments one of the males had made. Reynaldo had refused to cooperate with the breeding program.

The medic handed Carl a small container of pain killers and one of sedative pills, in case Reynaldo changed his mind. Then Carl started toward the new transports and the waiting panthran.

"It's a long trip," he said to the group. "We'll have food and water in the transport, so don't worry about bringing any. There are bathrooms on board too. Hopefully, you can sleep through most of it. Tomorrow, we'll be in Canada."

The group split up in preparation to leave, and Carl checked his communicator for any updates or messages. There was nothing important, so he tucked it in his pocket. He noticed Reynaldo watching him from across the way. It was hard to translate the look on his face. Carl didn't have much experience with mixed-species creations beyond rescuing them. With a nod, the panthran moved on to make sure his group was cared for.

The twenty-five panthran were divided up into two transports with two drivers each to split the shifts and two soldiers each in case they ran into trouble. Dan was assigned to supervise one vehicle and Carl the other.

"Take your pick," Dan said, checking his com one last time.

Carl noticed Reynaldo assisting a female into a transport and then preparing to get in himself. "I'll take that one." He jogged over and helped Reynaldo climb in without any more discomfort than necessary.

"Are the pain killers helping?" he asked as Reynaldo settled hesitantly into a seat.

"Yes. It's fine."

He wished Reynaldo had taken a sedative, but he understood the logic. The panthran was already looking around the transport and doing evaluations on the others.

Carl took a headcount. "Everyone's doing great."

Reynaldo smiled slightly, but didn't look convinced.

Across the field, Carl spotted the other group of ten

rescues from upstairs at the facility, loading into a third transport. It would travel separately from them, just in case. With more light, he could see they were all the cheetah/human mixed species: cheeman.

A soldier closed the back of their transport, and Carl and his portion of the panthran were sealed in. He felt the familiar hum of the engine and then lift of the vehicle as it prepared to leave camp.

The race to the border began now.

They hadn't risked arranging a safe route with troops for protection, wanting to keep the operation as covert as possible. One mole in the rebel army was all it took. Following the colonel's advice and general directions, they were on their own.

As they flew along, Carl thought back on Reynaldo's unsettling demand. Would he really be able to kill them if it came down to it? Would he be able to give an order to fire on Reynaldo—to blow him up? As a soldier, he knew the logic of it. If things at the facility had been violent and dangerous before, what would await them if they were recaptured?

But as a man, he was highly conflicted. How could he intentionally end the life of such remarkable creatures?

Of one specific remarkable creature.

Closing his eyes, Carl prayed. It wasn't something he turned to often, but they were going to need all the help they could get.

Please, let me be strong. Let us avoid Enforcers. Help me get these innocent lives safely to freedom.

THE FIRST BLAST WOKE THEM ALL. CARL'S HAND WAS ON HIS GUN before his eyes were open. Reynaldo shifted next to him, and cries of fear bounced around the cabin. Whatever the explosion was, it couldn't be good. Carl made eye contact with the other soldier, Private Nasab, at the far end near the door. She gave him a nod and pulled her gun across her lap.

A voice came over the radio. "Going dark."

The dim lights inside the transport went out. The windows were blocked, but it was procedure in case some glow slipped through the cracks in the door.

"Hold on," Carl whispered to the group. "It might get rough here for a bit." He tried to sound calm, but he was sure they could smell his agitation. Was it just a random roadblock or troops after them specifically?

The transport abruptly swerved to the right, and Reynaldo gasped in pain. One of the kits squealed and sobbed.

"The drivers are trained for this," Carl said. "Hang in there."

"Remember what I asked of you," Reynaldo hissed.

A chill ran up Carl's spine and tingled across his scalp. "I remember."

"Good. Keep your promise."

He'd hadn't actually promised to wipe out a whole clan of panthran. There had to be another way. A second explosion sounded, closer this time. Whoever was out there, the drivers weren't managing to evade them.

"Listen carefully," Carl said and felt the group go still in the darkness. "If we are hit or if we stop, stay together. Don't run away from the group unless you have no other choice. If you're separated, it will be harder for them to find you, but it will be hard for *us* too. Everyone on our team is trained for this moment. Stay with us."

A female whispered specific directions to her kit. Something about holding tight to her and not letting go. Adrenaline rushed through Carl's body, and he could only imagine the fear the panthran must be experiencing. Fight or flight or freeze was the instinctive response of all mammals. He prayed they could all stick with fight.

The transport flew along silently for several minutes before the vehicle slowed and then came to a complete stop.

A kit whimpered.

"Shhhh," a female panthran whispered.

Next to him in the silence, there was a wheeze to the inhale of Reynaldo's breathing. Conflicting emotions of wanting to rush the transport on its way for medical help and the reality of trusting the drivers to do their job wrestled in Carl's mind. He put a hand on Reynaldo's knee and squeezed gently. The panthran put his furry hand on top of Carl's and squeezed back, warmth spreading from it. Carl could feel the tension in the panthran's fingers as his claws extended and retracted slightly, instinctively responding to the stress.

Why does the one member of the group who would probably be the most useful in a fight have to be the only one with serious injuries? If Reynaldo wasn't so compromised, he'd be a force to be reckoned with. Maybe the guards at the facility had felt that as well and made sure to keep him in his place.

Carl checked his own breathing, pacing it slower than what he heard around him. He was grateful none of the creatures had become hysterical.

Reynaldo shifted nervously and clutched his hand tighter. The other panthran reacted as well with nervous shuffling—hearing something Carl couldn't. Reynaldo leaned closer and whispered, "Branches snapping. Someone's out there."

Carl nodded and gave the panthran's knee a solid grip before pulling away to get his gun ready. Laser rifle across his middle, he focused and exhaled into the moment, listening for any sign of attack. There was not a peep in the dark cabin. It was amazing the kits stayed so silent. Maybe a skill they'd learned early at the facility.

What felt like half an hour later, the engine vibrated with power.

"Hold on," he whispered as loudly as he dared, knowing what was coming. He braced for the escape a split second before the transport shot out of wherever it had been hidden.

A few panthran tumbled to the floor, and one rolled onto his foot. Pulling his ammo bag out of the way, he grabbed a furry arm or leg to keep the creature from further harm. No one made a sound as they raced through the night.

Finally, Carl's radio beeped, startling in the quiet cabin.

"That means we're clear," he said to the group. "They may keep the lights out for a while, but that's just a precaution."

He could hear the panthran regaining their seats, probably able to see to some extent, and Reynaldo relaxed next to him. After another ten minutes, the dim light was turned back on.

"Everyone okay?" Carl asked.

A few of the panthran nodded politely, but he was sure they were frightened. He wasn't all that calm himself.

"Try to relax and get some sleep now," he said, not sure what else to say.

"Can I take him to the bathroom?" a female asked, placing her hand on the back of the kit next to her.

"Of course."

A couple of others visited the restroom when the kit was done. Carl used the time to pass around some dried beef and a jug of water. The panthran talked among themselves, but he couldn't hear most of it. Reynaldo agreed to another round of pain pills, but Carl didn't even offer the sedative.

Once they were done eating and seemed settled again, Carl rested his head against the wall behind him. It would've been nice to have some kind of safe spot for a break along the way, but it wasn't worth the risk. Maybe, after a few more hours, they'd find some way to stretch in the cabin. He let the mild rumbling of the transport help him drift off to sleep.

It was still darkish in the cabin when Carl opened his eyes. Nothing seemed amiss, but he felt like something specific had woken him. Reynaldo was asleep, his head on Carl's shoulder. The soldier was grateful the panthran was able to rest, despite all the pain he must be in. Holding as still as possible so as not to wake him, Carl checked his com and listened for sounds outside the transport, but there was nothing. He tentatively closed his eyes again.

Then the world turned upside down.

CHAPTER 2

arl felt more than heard the explosion. His shoulders bashed into the ceiling. Then his body hit the floor and banged into others around him as the transport rolled several times and then flat-spun upside down.

Screams, roars, and hisses filled the cabin. Disoriented, Carl grabbed what felt like the metal bar of a storage rack. An alarm went off on his radio, but Carl couldn't reach it. One of the panthran was on top of him.

The transport stopped spinning and was still for a second. Carl tried to shout a warning, but he wasn't quick enough. The vehicle automatically righted itself, sending them all tumbling back to the floor.

Carl grabbed his radio and confirmed the red flashing light. They were in trouble.

Where is he? With broken ribs, being thrown around like that could've punctured Reynaldo's lungs.

He spotted the panthran near the back door, a tawny kit in each arm. Pain shone in his golden eyes, but he was breathing and alert. Nasab was checking on the panthran near her. Everyone appeared to be conscious. Other injuries would have to wait. He should have made them all strap in.

The engine turned off, and a tingle of fear ran across his skin. Carl grabbed his rifle from the seat where it had landed, glad it was in one piece and he'd had the safety on.

"Get behind me," he said firmly. "As far up toward the front as you can."

Led by Nasab, panthran quickly crawled past him, but Reynaldo didn't move.

"I can help," he said.

"I know, but *you* are what they want. Stay with your clan. Keep them safe."

Reynaldo glanced at the group of panthran huddled at the far end of the cabin and nodded slightly. He positioned himself between the group and the back door. Carl found his ammo bag and unzipped it, quickly grabbing another handgun and several explosive devices.

"Do you know how to use this?" he asked Reynaldo, showing him the gun.

"No."

"Well, here's how, then." In ten seconds, Carl whispered the basics on how to undo the safety, aim the laser dot, and pull the trigger. "Wait until they're fairly close. You don't have much range with this. Only use it if

Enforcers have gotten past us and are coming in the back of the vehicle. Otherwise, stay quiet and let us handle them."

Reynaldo stared at the gun, then glanced toward the back door of the transport.

"Stay in here," Carl said, sensing the protective alpha-male instinct rising up in the panthran. "My job is to keep you safe. Stay in the transport, and protect the group. That's how you can help the most."

Reynaldo tipped his head, but then nodded his consent. Two other males had moved up to crouch beside him. Carl considered giving them guns as well, but voices issuing orders came from outside the transport. He couldn't determine exactly what was going on, but it wasn't anything good.

The voices came around toward the back of the truck. Carl calmed his breathing, ready to respond, but the door stayed shut. Spotting a large tarp that had come out from under one of the seats during the roll, he had an idea. Unfolding it, he confirmed the tarp would be large enough. One of the males moved next to him, seeming to understand the plan.

"Cover yourselves up," Carl whispered. "It might buy me some time if they don't already know what our cargo is."

The male nodded and pulled the tarp back to the group. Carl could see that Reynaldo didn't want to hide, but with a frown, he pulled the tarp over himself as well. In the semi-darkness of the hold, it was impossible to tell what was under the covering. Unless they had dogs.

Carl's stomach clenched as he listened carefully. No barking. A good sign.

Two thumps sounded on the back door. Routine code from the driver that he was opening it up. *Better than a blast or gunfire,* Carl decided.

He tucked his gun just out of sight and sat back on the seat. Nasab followed his lead.

"Don't move, and stay quiet," he whispered to the hiding panthran, though it probably wasn't necessary. They knew what was at stake.

The door creaked open. Carl blinked at the sunlight flooding in. Blocking his eyes with one hand, Carl swallowed and barked, "What the fuck is going on out there?" The gold oak leaves on the collars of his Army fatigues showed he was a major. Maybe that would impress them.

"All transports are required to stop at checkpoints," a voice said. "Sir, can you please step out of the vehicle?"

"It's a good thing I can walk at all after taking that roll. Firing explosives at transports? Shit, I was sound asleep."

He stood, realizing he was going to have to leave his rifle behind. There was a small laser pistol tucked in the back of his pants that might come in handy, and he'd slipped an old-school grenade in each pocket. Nasab followed behind him, outwardly playing it cool. It took a moment for Carl's eyes to fully adjust to the midday sun so he could see better what they were up against. One of the drivers stood next to two young soldiers—privates, who both quickly saluted. A handful of other youngsters in uniform stood a few yards away. *This can't possibly be a team hunting for the escaped panthran.*

"Sorry about the blast, sir," the skinniest of them said. "We've had a lot of rebel activity in this area lately."

"As I'm sure the driver told you, we're not rebels. I needed a lift to a new assignment up north and caught a ride."

Pretending he was stretching an injured neck, Carl glanced around the area. He didn't see the other two transports or any other soldiers. So it was just the handful of them at an isolated checkpoint.

"What's under the tarp, sir?" the skinny private asked, craning his neck to look into the cabin.

"Just some supplies. Strapped down well, fortunately."

"Seems pretty tidy after that roll and spin you took," the soldier said.

Young, but not stupid. Fuck. "Lucky for you," Carl said. "General Carson likes his whiskey in one piece."

He hoped name-dropping and the suggestion of a valuable cargo would dissuade them. Carl realized the kid hadn't saluted him yet.

"I'll just take a look, sir, so I can fill out all the paperwork correctly."

Carl made eye contact with the driver, who gave an almost imperceptible nod of his head. Carl motioned grandly with his arm, like he welcomed the inspection. As two of the soldiers climbed into the hold, he simultaneously reached behind him for the gun with one hand and into his left pocket with the other.

The driver wrapped up the soldier near him from behind, forcing his arms to his side. Carl engaged and threw the grenade like a baseball toward the distant group of soldiers with his left hand. Before he could turn back to the transport, he heard the *schwep* of a laser gun. One private leaped from the vehicle, only to be met by Carl's gun blast. The skinny one fell out, already dead.

Looking into the hold, Carl saw Reynaldo peeking out from under the tarp, gun still aimed at the door. The driver had already dispatched the soldier he'd restrained, grabbed one of the Enforcer's guns, and was running to where the explosion had gone off. Laser blasts flashed, ending things for those who were only wounded. Private Nasab stood plastered against the open door of the transport, her eyes wide with fear. Maybe it was the first action she'd seen.

Sauntering back, the driver looked quite pleased with himself. He pulled out his radio. "All clear here. Did you get the checkpoint?"

"Affirmative," came through the radio. "Disabled communications and took it down."

"The other transport?" Carl asked, and the driver nodded. "Let's get moving again before someone comes to investigate."

Private Nasab climbed back in, but Carl paused a moment, staring at the dead soldiers on the ground around him. They were just kids. But the reality was that they had volunteered to be Enforcers and would have done their job, whatever that entailed for him—a traitor—and his charge of panthran. Shaking his head at the waste, Carl climbed back into the transport, and the driver closed the doors behind him.

"You can come out now," he said. "Grab spots quickly. We're gonna haul ass outta here."

The panthran all scrambled for seats, and he noticed several of them buckling in this time. Kits whimpered, and even Carl could smell their fear. Reynaldo took his seat next to Carl and handed the gun back.

"Good shot," Carl said.

"Wish I'd gotten them both. I'll have to practice my aim."

"Hopefully, you never need to do that again."

Carl didn't sense any regret from the panthran. Reynaldo had probably imagined killing an Enforcer for a long time—and not nearly so quickly and neatly.

The transport lurched to the air and then sped off, jostling the passengers.

"Did I hear the other group is safe?" Reynaldo asked.

"Yes. Everyone's safe."

"How much longer?" one of the females asked.

"Not sure," Carl admitted. "No idea where we are. And we might need to use a different route now. The military is going to notice when that group doesn't report in."

The female nodded but looked scared.

"It will be over soon," Reynaldo said to assure her.

Carl hoped he was right. The drivers knew what their options were. They didn't want to die today either. It felt like the transport was going at a ridiculous speed, but the sooner they cleared that area, the better. Coded messages were probably going back and forth between the three transports.

Carl tried to relax and let the other rebel soldiers do their jobs. He'd done his. All his panthran were still alive.

"Is anyone injured?" Carl asked the group.

No one responded. He hoped they weren't just being stoic. Not like there was much he could do about an injury at that point.

"Only bumps and bruises," one of the males finally said.

⸻◆⸻

After a few more hours of travel, they began to stir, and snacks were passed around. Reynaldo agreed to another round of pain killers, but no sedatives. If anything, he'd been proved right about needing to stay alert and clear-headed.

Most of the panthran weren't interested in talking to Carl, but the kits were curious about him, patting his thick, curly hair and discussing it with their mothers in a language Carl didn't recognize. There were some words to it, but also hisses and growls and chirps—like languages in Africa with tongue clicks that always amazed him.

"I guess you could call it panthranese," Reynaldo said.

"We made it up ourselves so the guards wouldn't know what we were saying."

Fascinating. People who saw genetic creations as animals would never believe they could create their own language.

"How long had you lived at that facility?" Carl asked. "We can't find accurate records because it technically doesn't exist."

"I was born there. A natural birth, but my parents are dead now. I'm not sure exactly how old I am. Days and years blend together. I'm considered an adult, ready to breed for many years."

"Mixed species physically mature faster than humans," Carl said. "Tigran are considered adults of breeding age at only thirteen."

"Humans can't breed that young?"

"I guess some can biologically, but it's certainly not healthy or considered morally right. They're still children themselves. Humans don't stop growing until they're eighteen or nineteen. Even that is considered young for having children. Most women wait until they're well into their twenties or thirties."

"That's a long time to wait to copulate."

Carl burst out a laugh at that word choice. "I doubt they hold out that long. Even married couples wait to bring children into the world."

"How do they wait for children? If you copulate, the offspring will happen."

"They get a special shot or use a birth control device to prevent that."

"Oh. Our females are not offered that choice."

Carl nodded. *Of course not.* They were expected to breed as often as possible. No one was going to delay the arrival of new panthran kits, though exactly what the long-term goal was—why they were keeping them hidden away in cages—he didn't understand.

After a few minutes of companionable silence, Reynaldo turned his deep-golden gaze back to the soldier. "So, you and your mate, do you have young ones?"

"No mate yet," Carl admitted. "And no young ones."

Reynaldo's whiskers flared, and his eyes grew wide in his black furry face. "No mate? You are an excellent candidate."

Carl felt his cheeks flush, though it wouldn't show through his own dark skin. "I suppose, but I've never found one enticing enough. You don't have a mate either, from what I hear."

"No, but that's for different reasons."

Carl felt like his heart skipped a beat, and his chest clenched. A small part of him began to wonder if Reynaldo's refusal to breed or select a mate had the same source as his own mate-less status. Had the Enforcers suspected the same thing? Another reason for the whippings and beatings? Reynaldo wasn't more forthcoming than that, and Carl didn't want to ask or answer any more direct questions that could lead to dangerous answers.

Their eyes met, and the panthran slow-blinked—a

feline action Carl understood to mean friendship and acceptance. He gave a small nod in return. Letting the subject rest there, they watched the kits across from them cuddling with their mothers.

"Those kits are pretty adorable, though," Carl said. Not enough to want a human version for himself, but still adorable.

He let the gentle hum of the transport and the warmth of Reynaldo's body next to his lull him back into sleep. He only woke when the transport slowed again. Before he could panic, a message came through his com that they were pulling up to the camp in Winnipeg. The stealthy border crossing into Canada must have gone smoothly, or he'd slept through that stop, which he doubted.

"We're there," he announced.

The atmosphere shifted from tension to excited chattering. Voices came from outside the transport, but these sounded calm and were issuing directions—not barking and angry, like the soldiers who'd attacked them. When they came to a full stop, someone banged twice and opened the back door to their transport. Private Nasab hopped out immediately to help the rest of them down.

Carl stood to assure the panthran all was well. "Welcome to Canada! There's a team here to take care of you now. I'll escort you to the medical tent for check-in and any necessary care." He glanced back at Reynaldo, who smiled and rested a hand on the bandaging wrapped around his middle.

"But you'll stay with us?" one of the females whispered.

He understood her fears. His presence was one they could trust.

"For a while, but my job is done. You've made it to safety. There are dozens of people here ready to support you and get you settled into your new life. I'm sure the Army has another assignment waiting for me. Sadly, you're not the only ones being held captive."

Turning to Reynaldo, he tried to pass the reins a bit. The panthran seemed to understand and stood up, wincing in pain.

"Let's meet back up with the others and find out what comes next," Reynaldo said.

One of the kits frowned up at him. "You need to see a doctor."

"I'm sure we can take care of that now," Reynaldo assured him.

Carl climbed out of the transport, his legs barely cooperative after so long in the vehicle. Private Nasab helped lift the kits out, and one panthran after another set their feet on safe Canadian soil. Reynaldo was the last one out, and he joined the others in gaping at the new world around them.

Carl understood the feeling. He still marveled at the size of the environmental dome—the largest in the world, covering ten square miles—that kept everyone inside safe and away from the elements of the imminent Canadian winter. The ceiling two football fields above them gave a sense of being outside in the open. Carl expected the kits to be frightened, but they seemed more amazed. Besides Reynaldo, had any of them ever been out of the dank basement lab? Getting acclimated would take some adjusting.

During Carl's last visit, the rebels were still working on transferring the facility from an agricultural research station to a refugee camp. He was flabbergasted by the progress in just a few weeks. A huge medical tent was set up near the entrance, ready to evaluate and register new arrivals. There were several large buildings that looked administrative, and rows of small bamboo houses had been set up, resembling the start of a small city. The arrival grounds near the entrance were still wide open and would probably stay that way, but there was a small fire pit and meeting area nearby that had already been well used. He spotted the other panthran transport and the third transport of the cheeman. They had all made it.

"This way, please," a woman in a nurse's uniform said, motioning toward the medical tent.

"I need a toilet," a kit whispered to his mother.

"Over there," the nurse said, pointing out a small shack. "Then join us in the tent so we can get you checked in. Okay?"

The kit smiled hesitantly up at her, then he and his mother walked slowly to the restroom. The other panthran moved cautiously in the direction of the medical tent.

"Be gentle with them," Carl said to the nurse. "They've been through a lot. Our species has not been kind to them, to say the least."

"We will. That's the state of nearly every creature we've seen so far. A few have been families escaping the Gathering, but so many come from secret labs. Humans disgust me."

Carl frowned at that. "Yes, we are a pretty disgusting species, altogether."

He followed the nurse into the medical tent and confirmed that each panthran was settling in on a cot. Most were happy to lie down and be still. It had been a long, stressful journey. He spotted Reynaldo a few cots down and smiled in his direction. The panthran was on his side, probably protecting the wounds on his back, and he smiled in return. Someone had already removed his temporary bandaging, so Carl hoped he'd be stitched up and taken care of soon.

"Who we have here?" a tiny Asian doctor said, pulling a cart bigger than herself up to Reynaldo's cot. "Bad guys made a mess of you, that for sure."

Carl worried her bluntness might be too much, but Reynaldo smiled.

"I'm Agnus," the doctor said. "You all the first panthrans I ever see with own eyes."

The idea that this doctor didn't know what she was doing worried Carl, so he hurried over to the cot.

"Name?" Agnus asked.

"Reynaldo."

"Last name?"

"Don't have one. Hasn't been needed."

"Humph." Agnus snorted and started pulling implements off her cart. "Let me get blood for tests. You too skinny. We fatten you up quick. Lots of good food and vitamins."

Carl watched as she did some scans and general checks. In the bright light of the medical tent, the rosette spots under the black of Reynaldo's fur peeked out. The panthran was still covered with a blanket below the waist, and Carl was grateful. The less detailed information he carried with him about this stunning male, the better for his own peace of mind. Mental images of Reynaldo whole and healthy were already problematic.

"Now, that back. Very bad."

Agnus started to roll him over more onto his stomach, but Carl shouted for her to stop.

"Broken ribs," Carl said while Reynaldo gritted his teeth in pain.

Agnus paused and sat down in a chair so she was eye-level with Reynaldo on the cot.

"You come from very bad place. You never should be treated bad. You hear me? No more bad here. You say when hurt. You say NO. You in charge of own body now."

Reynaldo nodded, holding his ribs carefully.

"I need to help, but help may hurt some. Okay? Maybe you sit up so I can see whole back?"

Carl held out a hand, and Reynaldo took it, allowing Carl to assist him to a sitting position.

"Not much to do for ribs," Agnus said. "We get X-ray on those soon and see, but usually heal on they own eventually."

"Always have," Reynaldo agreed.

"How many times you had broke ribs?" Agnus asked with a glower on her face.

Reynaldo thought about it. "Four times, maybe five."

Agnus mumbled some words in another language.

"What's that?" Carl asked with a smile.

"Oh, those not nice words," she said, fussing around on the cart and preparing a syringe with some fluid. "I not even know how say in English." She showed Reynaldo the needle. "This *strong* pain killer. May make you sleepy or dizzy, but help you get through next few hours better. Okay?"

"Okay," Reynaldo agreed, probably too tired to fight about it and glad for some serious pain relief.

For Carl, the agreement meant Reynaldo felt safe. That was more important than just about anything else.

Agnus injected the medication into his hip and then prepared wraps and fluids to clean up his wounded back. Moving around behind him, she paused, her angry expression shifting to pity and then back to an even fiercer anger. Mumbling more unknown curses under her breath, Agnus began to wash and use antiseptic on the angry red welts. The panthran grumbled something in panthranese, and Carl suspected it was a version of swearing as well.

Others from the group were preparing to head on to the next steps, and Carl could sense they were hesitant to leave the tent without Reynaldo.

"How much longer do you think?" Carl asked the doctor.

"Too late for stitches. Already some healing. So much scar tissue. Big hairy mess."

Reynaldo shrugged. "Nobody ever stitched anything up before."

She huffed and cursed some more. "We need take you to hospital for X-ray. See how ribs doing, make sure lungs not injured, and wrap you up."

"Wrap me up in what?" Reynaldo asked.

Carl left them to discuss treatment options and went to talk with the group of new refugees.

"Reynaldo needs more time with the doctor," he said, "and he may need to stay in the hospital for a bit. There are many workers here who will help you find your new homes and get settled in."

As the group hesitated, a female tigran wearing the uniform of a camp guard—khakis and a belt with a radio attached—approached them with a friendly fang-filled smile.

"Welcome, friends," she said brightly.

The kits hid behind their mothers, and the whole group visibly compressed together. Had they ever seen a tigran before? Or was she just too cheerful? Ignoring their reaction, the guard continued.

"My name is Nimmy, and I'm going to help you find

your homes and make sure everything you need is there. Clothes and food and other supplies are being delivered right now. Let's find your unit numbers," she said, looking at her clipboard.

"Clothes?" one of the kits said in horror. "We have to wear clothes? Like humans?"

The kit seemed oblivious of the fact that the tigran in front of him was fully dressed. There was a base level of "civilized" expected in the camp.

Carl smiled at the guard. "I'll let you handle that issue. Good luck."

He turned back to see Agnus helping Reynaldo up from the cot. His back was now a mass of white bandaging that was loosely wrapped in place with gauze.

Reynaldo looked over to him with sad golden eyes, and Carl wished he could make the next few days whoosh by—the pain while the panthran healed and the stress of settling into a new life.

But what awaited all of the refugees? Even if the rebels won the war, could they live among humans? Tigran had done that successfully for generations, but it wasn't ending well for them now.

As the panthran congregation followed Nimmy down the main road toward their new houses, a cart driven by a medic pulled up outside the tent. Agnus watched as Reynaldo headed toward it, but she was shaking her head and probably still swearing.

Carl wondered which job was harder. His of being on

the rescue end of things or hers of trying to patch up the mess humans made of their own genetic creations?

Reynaldo reached him, but he was moving tentatively. Probably woozy from the drugs.

"Hang in there," Carl said. "The next few days may be rough, but you'll get through it."

"My family is safe now. That's really all that matters." He started to climb into the waiting cart, but then he paused and looked at the ground. "Are you staying here, at the camp?"

"I doubt it," Carl said. "At some point, I'm sure I'll end up here. My cover will be blown, or they'll need me here instead of in the field. But for now, I'm likely off to the next assignment."

"That's too bad," Reynaldo said. "Well, at least for me."

Carl's stomach did a downright pubescent flutter. Even if he was reading meaning into that comment, staying with Reynaldo was a thousand times more appealing than heading back out into his double-agent life. But there was a war going on and creatures to be saved. The rest would have to wait.

"I hope you're back soon," Reynaldo said. "I should be more presentable by then. Definitely smell better."

They both chuckled, and Carl reached out his hand. Reynaldo shook it, finally looking up. When their eyes met, Carl swallowed down a dozen things he wanted to say. Like, *I already know I'm going to think about you every day. Worry about you. Imagine . . .*

"I look forward to that," he said instead, adding his other hand on top of Reynaldo's dark furry one.

Reluctantly letting go, Carl waited as the panthran eased himself onto the cart seat, waving as it drove off to the hospital. Carl watched until it was out of sight.

Everything in him wanted to ask for a transfer, to stay at the camp, but he knew the rebel army had trained him for a much higher purpose. And maybe he'd misunderstood Reynaldo's gratitude for something it wasn't. Digging deep for his sense of honor and duty, Carl turned away and headed into the administration building.

"Ah, Major Thompson," a private behind the main desk said, standing and saluting sharply. "We've been waiting for you. Excellent job on the successful rescue."

"Thank you," Carl said, returning the salute half-heartedly.

"Sir, are you injured?"

Carl glanced down and realized there were brown smears several places on his uniform. Reynaldo's blood. His throat caught for a moment.

"It's not mine."

The private nodded with wide eyes, then motioned to a nearby door. "Right this way."

She led him to a conference room, where the rescue team was relaxing with snacks and quiet conversations. They started to rise, but he quickly motioned them to stay at ease.

"Major," a plain-clothed woman in the far corner said. "I have your new orders."

Heading her direction, Carl noticed manila envelopes on the table in front of each of the team members. They must be splitting up, otherwise he would've been the one handing out new assignments. Maybe he'd be staying at the camp after all. With Reynaldo. Images of what that might lead to flashed through his mind, but he shook them off.

The woman handed him his envelope, and he opened it straightaway. After reading through, he stopped and scanned the room. None of the rest of the team seemed agitated or worried, so he sensed they weren't headed the same place as him. Then his eyes met Dan's, who appeared stressed and downright scared. Carl nodded slightly, and Dan returned the nod. It looked like they might be venturing together into a precarious situation. One that would likely end with their covers being blown wide open.

Satellites had discovered a massive hidden facility deep in the Colorado mountains. No one was exactly sure what was going on there, but tigran and other creatures had been documented entering and not coming back out again. As many as a hundred of them. Carl's next mission was to go in as a soldier of the U.S. Army—the one currently led by President Kerkaw as commander in chief —but actually undercover to gather intelligence and be an inside source before the rebel troops attacked and freed the prisoners there. Much more complicated and dangerous than just the smash-and-grab rescues he'd done so far.

Looking at the images, Carl wondered what he would find in a facility that looked to be an old ski resort. He realized everyone in the room was staring at him.

"Excellent job, team," he said formally. "You completed the mission flawlessly, even when it seemed like the whole thing was going tits-up. Thank you for your service. You are dismissed to your next assignment."

No one moved for a moment, and the soldiers looked at each other in confusion. Finally, one spoke.

"Sir," she said, "aren't you coming with us to join up with the troops in Chicago?"

"No," Carl said, catching Dan's eye. "But I'm sure you will have an excellent commanding officer going forward."

"Where are you assigned?" a driver asked.

"Another rescue?" Private Nasab asked, looking a bit jealous to be left out.

"Sorry. That's classified."

⸺⸻◆⸻⸺

CARL AND DAN HAD NOT BEEN PREPARED FOR THE HORRORS OF the facility they'd entered undercover. The old ski resort was much more than a simple research and development location. They had to stand by silently for months while mixed-species females were raped and abused, offspring were separated from their parents and used as leverage, females like Taliya were impregnated (through coercion and threat), and any creature who dared stand up for themselves or their family was swiftly eliminated or stuffed in the dank underground dungeon. The day rebel forces arrived and helped free the captive creatures was one of the proudest moments of Carl's life.

It also brought him back to the refugee camp, reuniting with Reynaldo.

CHAPTER 3

Reynaldo had lived outside of the facility's dungeon during his years working with the military equestrian team, but even for him, the transition to life in the refugee camp was shocking. Once the panthran were past the initial health exams and check-ins, no one studied them, stuck them with needles, or monitored anything about their daily life. They were divided into ten separate houses, given food and clothing (which they were expected to wear), and then left on their own.

While he didn't need to spend the night in the hospital, Rey had arrived with serious injuries and was supposed to rest and recover before joining life in the camp. He had several cracked ribs and wounds to heal. But he did manage to join the other panthran in exploring the massive dome and adjusting to what felt like open, outdoor sky and air.

Rey had been assigned to a two-bedroom unit with

three other panthran males, but the humans running the camp made it clear it didn't matter if they moved around as long as they let administration know for their records. So much freedom of choice was daunting. More than half of the panthran tended to stay in their units, used to that life of being in one place.

Learning to use the shower, getting accustomed to clothes (though most snuck around without shoes), and figuring out how to prepare meals from the food provided was enough of a shock to their systems. Beds and laundry and so many "civilized" details to figure out. There were humans they could talk to if it was all too much, but none of the panthran had any interest in broadcasting their distress. The humans mostly stuck to the front portion of camp and let the creatures have the rest for themselves. A group of female liran living on the same row supported the new arrivals better, probably because they'd also come from a lab and had experienced the same culture shock and adjustment.

Three days after their arrival, Nimmy the tigran showed up on Rey's doorstep with a list of jobs in camp he could select from. Crops needed tending, food and supplies had to be distributed daily, and a school was being established. After reviewing his options, Rey chose assisting in the refugee school.

When he'd worked with the military, he learned to read, something few lab creatures could do. He wasn't as proficient as an adult human, but fluent enough to help with the youngest arrivals. And it was a chance to improve his own skills. There was a small library at camp, and he was excited to check out the offerings. He also agreed to help with the new arrivals of freed creatures and supplies. If there'd been a choice involving animals, that would have been more interesting, but the goats used for food were kept at a different location nearby.

Over the weeks, the panthran settled into their new lives. There was work to do and a steady flow of new arrivals—mostly tigran families escaping the Gathering. Entertainment nights were set up in the new school, which had a media wall, and they all learned about movies, news broadcasts, and old comedy shows. None of that was new for Rey, but he had definitely missed the distraction media brought. He loved seeing his panthran friends laugh and relax into their freedom.

One morning in early March, the camp all but vibrated with the news of a massive rescue. Rey could feel the excitement before he even stepped out the door. Young ones ran up and down the streets, and humans were busy preparing. It wasn't unexpected. Teams had been racing to put up new housing units in anticipation. But no one had known exactly when it would happen. Breaking into a run, Rey reached the open area at the front of camp as devices were being handed out to the regular work crew.

"At least a hundred creatures," he overheard Nimmy say.

Rey froze. "A *hundred?*"

Nimmy turned to him and nodded with wide eyes.

"One of the biggest facilities we've ever captured. Full rebel army attack and demolition!"

She stepped back to address the team. "We're setting up the new houses with food and bedding, but more supplies will need to be sorted once we know exactly who we have. Reports include not only tigran and liran but cheeman and even berman."

Rey's tail puffed at that idea. *How huge would a berman be?*

"Our insider spies have given us a basic idea of family grouping," Nimmy continued, "but we will need to be flexible and work with the new arrivals."

The rest of that day was a blur: loading food boxes, sorting clothing for various sizes, and helping sweep and tidy the new housing units. Samson—the enormous liger/tigran hybrid called a ligran—calmly and efficiently instructed medical personnel, supplies distribution, and those in charge of leading the new refugees from one check-in spot to another. It was the first time Rey would be greeting a large group coming from a terrible situation, reflecting his own panthran clan and their arrival at the camp. He was determined to be welcoming and support-ive. When the transports pulled in through the huge front gates late in the day, Rey mostly held back and waited to be given directions by the administrators in charge.

The back of the newest transport opened, and a large family of cheeman hesitantly climbed out. Rey wondered if he should head that way since he'd be working with the young ones at the school.

A distinctive scent caught his attention. Unmistakable. *He's here.*

Two transports over, Carl stood talking with a group of three orange tigran and a white male with what looked like a pure-white kit in his arms. Rey stared, his heart racing, as Carl led the tigran to the medical tent. The soldier stooped to reassure the two young orange tigran, who both looked terrified. Coming from a facility, it was easy to imagine they were not fans of doctors and medical exams. Reynaldo felt like his insides were melting at the sight of the hulk of a man comforting the scared kits—as compassionate and caring as he'd been throughout the panthran rescue.

"That is Major Thompson," Samson mentioned to Nimmy as he pointed toward Carl. "One of our eyes inside for months. Since his loyalty is now revealed, he will be staying with us. I have assigned him to Section Three after a few days of rest."

He's staying! Rey's claws flexed in and out involuntarily, and he took a deep breath to calm himself. *He's staying.*

Watching through the mass of furry bodies, the panthran could only imagine the battle that had been fought to free so many creatures. He waited until the soldier passed off his charges to the process, drawing near as Carl signed forms on a device and spoke with Samson, who headed into the medical tent.

After being undercover in what must have been a horrible facility for so long, Carl might not even remember one creature among hundreds he'd helped. He looked exhausted, a heavy layer of black stubble on his face where he'd been clean-shaven before. He smelled as expected after a battle, overnight on the road, and close quarters with others in the transport. Yet under it all lingered that unique scent Rey had woken imagining next to him more than one night.

"Welcome back, soldier."

Carl turned, fatigue creasing his eyebrows together. Seeing Rey, he looked confused for a moment. Then recognition (and maybe something more) flashed in his eyes.

"Wow! Look at you, all civilized and official."

Rey adjusted the collar on his khaki tunic and smiled, fangs and all. "You get used to it, after a while."

Carl chuckled. "Camp life is clearly doing you wonders. All healed up?"

Their eyes met, and Rey swallowed down several thoughts about how the soldier should check for himself. Thoroughly. "Yes. All better."

"Reynaldo?" Nimmy called. "You're up!"

They both turned her direction, and Rey waved to acknowledge her.

"Sounds like you're all settled in, part of the team," Carl said with a tired grin.

"They keep us busy." He only had moments. Disoriented and confused refugees would be waiting for him outside of medical. *He's staying. There's no rush. Right?* "I heard you'll be joining the team as well now."

Carl blew out a breath. "Yep. My cover is well and

truly blown. Guess I'm here for support until they send me off to fight with the rebels."

"Then I'll see you around. Hopefully." Rey concentrated on regulating his breathing. Not like a human would necessarily read that as another creature would.

Carl tipped his head with a smirk. "Absolutely."

"Major Thompson?" another soldier called into the crowd.

Carl gave Reynaldo a wink. "No rest for the wicked. Catch ya later." He saluted jauntily and jogged off toward the sound of his summons.

Rey's hackles spiked slightly as he watched him go, suddenly worried he'd been too friendly or not enough. Movement near the medical tent caught Reynaldo's eye, and he spotted a group of female liran standing with Nimmy, clustered together and looking petrified—hackles raised, ears back, and eyes wide. Waiting for him to welcome them into this new life. Everything else would have to wait, but an urgency for Carl's presence simmered under Rey's skin.

⊰•——◆——•⊱

As Reynaldo headed back toward the front of camp half an hour later, the fake sun overhead dimmed. He wondered if they'd leave some light until the whole group was processed. Hurrying over to give his support, Rey reached the social area and campfire to find a crowd buzzing with excitement.

"What's happening?" he asked the closest guard.

"A handfasting for two new arrivals, to keep the family together."

Rey had no idea what that meant, but he couldn't see Nimmy or anyone waiting outside of medical. That part of welcoming the arrivals seemed complete, so he wandered over to the campfire. It was hard to see past the circle of creatures, but it looked like the two adult tigran Carl had talked with earlier were preparing for a formal ceremony with Samson. All three kits stood by them, and Rey wondered if they were a family who'd been together at the facility.

"Kano and Taliya," Samson said loudly, "as your hands are joined together, so may your hearts always be. Taliya, do you agree to be handfast with this tigran? To be his mate for the rest of your life, to care for the kits you may bear, and to support him in all of his endeavors?"

Rey realized it was a wedding, of sorts, probably as much as genetic creations were allowed. He couldn't hear the response, but everyone was smiling so it must be a yes.

A familiar deep sigh and distinctive smell made Rey's skin tingle. Carl stood next to him.

"Aww, good on them," Carl said.

Rey glanced over, and they exchanged comfortable smiles. The panthran felt confident this human was his friend. He'd remembered Rey. In that crowd, Carl had chosen to stand next to him. It wasn't enough, but it would do.

The white tigran agreed to the bond, and the kits were included as well. Rey felt an *aww* himself, even though he didn't know the creatures. A mental image of standing with Carl in a handfasting in front of Samson like that made his breath catch. *Impossible.*

"And you," Samson called out, "tigran and others too, will you honor this ceremony and treat their union and their family with the respect it is due?"

Cheers and calls of "aye" and "yes" went up in a blast of sound that made Rey jump. Carl hooted next to him and raised a fist in celebration.

"This union that began under cruel circumstances will now come out into the world by choice," Samson boomed loudly enough for the whole medical tent to hear. "We are all witnesses to it and will fight to see that this family remains intact, together, and will never be divided by any force on this earth."

Samson performed something ceremonial with a rope around their hands and said, "Kano and Taliya are now handfast. The knot joining them is tied."

The couple whispered to each other and kissed. The crowd cheered again, and a male liran played rapid notes on a guitar, the kind of music you felt inside. Rey had never danced, but he was confident that's what you were supposed to do. Yet no one did. The crowd went back to their conversations and bottles of ale. Rey was suddenly aware of Carl standing close enough that they touched from shoulder to hand. A tigran bumped them, rushing past in the excitement, and the connection was broken.

"I should go get cleaned up," Carl said, brushing off the front of his uniform.

"Have they shown you to your house yet?"

"No." Carl pulled a piece of paper from his pocket. "But I have the unit number."

"I can help you find it," Rey said, forcing his voice not to shake. "It's part of what I do here."

Carl motioned exaggeratedly toward the path into the housing area. "Let's go."

Rey checked the unit number on the paper and pointed the way. Everyone was out and about with the new arrivals, and the streets were crowded. The pair walked in silence, trying to avoid running into creatures who were busy organizing or trying to find their footing in the new place.

"Here it is," Rey said. "District Three, Unit 314."

Carl gave the bamboo building a quick appraisal and nodded. They both stood awkwardly for a few seconds as the crowd milled around them. Then the door to Unit 314 flew open, and another soldier holding a brown bottle smiled at them.

"Come on, man. Cold ale in the fridge. Hot water in the shower. Hoo-ah!"

"Roger that," Carl said.

The soldier headed back inside, where several other men celebrated on the couch. Rey struggled to translate the scents he was receiving from Carl. Mostly unfamiliar. Rey felt guilty, keeping him from enjoying the end of what surely had been a stressful and exhausting mission.

"Well," the panthran said, "see you later."

Carl hesitated. Frowned. Looked at the people already inside the unit. "Yeah. I should head in." His deep-brown eyes met Rey's dark-golden ones. "I'm not sure what they have planned for me here, but I will definitely find you. *Soon.* Okay?"

Rey flared his whiskers. "Okay." Carl's words were so pointed and precise. Said so carefully. It felt meaningful beyond a *see you around.* "Most days, I'm at the school."

Carl tapped the panthran's hand, smiled, then headed inside to be met by the shouts and cheers of his brothers-in-arms. Rey stared through the doorway for a solid minute—his hand all but vibrating where the man had touched him—until someone swung it shut.

⸎

REY DIDN'T SEE CARL AGAIN FOR TWO DAYS. HE FOUND THE panthran sorting supplies for the new arrivals. Rey looked up to discover the soldier standing across the table from him—clean, shaved, and in a camp guard khaki uniform.

"Hey," he said, trying to sound calm. Act civilized. Not like he'd been obsessing about how to reconnect with Carl for the last forty-eight hours.

"What do ya think?" Carl said, re-tucking his shirt. "Guess I'm officially here for a while."

"I'd say you'll blend right in, but there's no chance of that."

Rey hoped it came across as a compliment. The look in Carl's eyes suggested it had.

"I think I slept through my whole first day here," Carl said with a one shoulder shrug. "Now I've finally got the basic lay of the land. It's developed so much since last time."

For a moment, his smile faded, and Rey acknowledged with a nod that the last time had been his own arrival. A dark time that felt so far away now. Another life.

"And I made it through all the training meetings. Finally have a second to myself." Carl shifted his stance, and Rey could have sworn he smelled nervous. "So, will you have some time later to show me around? Give me the insider tour?"

It seemed illogical that Carl needed a tour guide. His eyes met Rey's, and a rush of pheromones hit the panthran, tingling all the way down his spine. No one—human or hybrid—had ever responded like that to his presence. Rey set down the pile of towels he'd been mindlessly holding.

"Um, yes." Rey glanced at the table. "I have to . . ."

"Let me help, and you can get done faster."

In an hour, the pair left the commissary shed and wandered the streets of the camp. They talked about new developments here and there, but Rey found it complicated to notice anything except the dozen seemingly intentional times when Carl's hand brushed his own or he placed a strong hand in the middle of the panthran's back as they moved through a crowd.

Rey had wondered—hundreds of times over the last months—if Carl was different, like him. When he was a teen and first beginning to understand mating, Rey had never comprehended the appeal of what was expected. Breeding more black panthran was his main duty at the facility where he was born. But the only coupling that had sparked his interest was with another male, who did *not* share his attraction. When the scientists noticed, Rey was beaten. He learned to keep those feelings to himself.

But when he was sent to the equine facility, he'd discovered there were enough males who were only interested in mating with other males (and females with other females) for there to be laws making it illegal. Punishable by death, not just a whipping.

So while nothing made him happier than Carl's attentions, he knew better than to initiate any of the multitude of physical things he longed to. Carl was here now. For a while, apparently. And that was enough. Having a friend would have to be enough.

When they reached the far end of the environmental dome, the pair stopped at the expanse of freshly broken ground that was going to be an enormous building.

"I'm hoping they bring some livestock in here," Rey said. "I loved working with horses, but there's no opportunity for that so far."

"If animals that you want to care for end up here, I will make it happen. But I'm sure the school appreciates your help. The kits will need to be ready for life in the world after the war."

"I try not to think about that. Living out in the world." Rey sighed. "When I sort of did that before, I loved the horses, but not the humans around me. They just saw me as another animal." He rubbed the scar running from ear to shoulder, remnants of a well-aimed whip. "A monster. Treated me like one too."

Carl turned to face him. "I don't see you that way."

"I know. That's why we can be friends."

"Friends." Carl frowned and swallowed. "So . . . Listen . . ."

Rey was alarmed by the level of nervous energy flowing from the soldier. Maybe he didn't really want to have any relationship. He was just bored. A new arrival. Trying to be nice.

"I understand." Rey looked down and flexed his claws. "But it was nice spending time with you today."

Carl grabbed Rey's hand with both of his own. "No, wait."

Rey looked up at him, the warmth from Carl's touch making his knees weak.

"I can settle for that," Carl said. "But I want to make sure we're clear."

"About what?"

"You refused to breed with the females."

Rey's ears lowered, embarrassment over failure. "Yeah."

"So it makes me wonder if your feelings on the subject are more like mine."

Another wave of pheromones and testosterone hit the

panthran, and he struggled to breathe. He'd been right in his suspicions. His hopes. Not that it mattered in the end. "I . . . you . . . You shouldn't talk about things like that."

"You've been beaten for it," Carl said, frowning.

"Repeatedly. It's against the law. I was too valuable to kill, or they would have."

"But now you're in Canada."

"How's that different?"

Carl smiled and squeezed Rey's hand. "Preferring males is not against the law. Not even humans and creatures as mates is illegal."

"Oh." The panthran's stomach fluttered with panic and excitement. Carl was still holding his hand. Standing so close. "There are relationships like that? Here?" He'd certainly never seen any.

"I'm not saying it happens often, but it's not breaking any rule. No one here will be punished for it."

Rey's tail puffed, and he forced himself not to pant— suddenly intensely aware they were alone at this currently unused end of the dome, a mile away from anyone else. Holding hands. The intimacy he'd dreamed about many times.

"If you would like to be more than friends," Carl said, "I really want that. Been thinking about it for months. Since there are so many Americans in camp, I asked the people in charge. It's okay."

Now Rey was sure he was going to pass out. Carl wanted to be with him enough to have had that dangerous conversation with camp administrators. Admitted things about himself that the Army would now know. It was too much to process.

"But if I'm wrong," Carl continued, dropping Rey's hand, "I don't want to make you uncomfortable."

Carl leaned back a bit. Giving Rey space. The panthran felt it for the moment it was. He could let the man keep moving away, or stop him.

Rey grabbed Carl's hand back, looking down at it, and shifted closer. "You're not wrong. I have been thinking about it for months too. But I don't . . . I've never . . ."

Carl tipped the panthran's face up to meet his eyes and smiled. "It's okay. That's all we need to know right now."

Rey leaned in and rested his forehead against Carl's. For that moment, their breathing fell together rhythmically, the scent of the soldier's longing for him filling his senses. He needed to be as clear in response. Show how desperately he desired this man who'd risked so much to be together.

Tilting his head, Rey touched his lips to Carl's. The electric-like shock of it made him gasp and lean back. Carl touched his face again and smiled before pulling him in for a gentle kiss that instantly made everything right. Full of unlimited potential. Rey sighed and rested his head on Carl's shoulder.

"Never again," Carl whispered. "No one's ever going to hurt you ever again."

That was the start of what they both soon agreed would be forever. Somehow. Somewhere.

It was complicated to find private time. They both lived in houses and shared bedrooms with other men. And both agreed keeping what Carl called PDA low-key was best. But there were storage closets and quiet rooms here and there. Media nights for movies. Evenings around the campfire, where Carl played the guitar and Rey learned they both sang very well. They'd petitioned the administration for a living unit to themselves, but that was difficult, even for some long-time tigran partners. But none of that mattered much.

They believed they had decades ahead of them. Together.

CHAPTER 4

The transport bringing Carl one step closer to Rey and his kidnappers glided on, though not nearly fast enough for General Thompson's liking. Too much time to torture himself anew over what his mate had been suffering for years. The broken promise made after their first kiss, that nothing would ever hurt him again. Carl had arranged animals for the panthran to care for with the dragons and other rescued hybrids, but he hadn't kept the love of his lifetime safe from harm.

If he closed his eyes, Carl could relive watching the video of the breach at the refugee camp and every raw emotion that came with it. The bone-cold terror seeing Rey collapse in the middle of the dragon training arena, shot with a tranquilizer. Being unceremoniously dragged through a hole in the back of the environmental dome.

That was the last he'd seen of his beloved partner.

Over two years ago.

After endless meetings and debates, Carl had been given the green light to organize an Army team and storm the compound where Rey was being held prisoner. He desperately hoped the intelligence was correct and Rey was still alive. Today—June 1, 2176—the Army would set him free. Whatever it took.

The last year had shown that the kidnappers weren't going to let their prize go without a violent fight. Carl breathed slowly, forcing his heartrate down, but his chest still felt constricted, his stomach roiled. It could churn all it wanted. There was no way he was sitting out this rescue mission.

Luckily, the driver next to him was not the chatty type. Being a commanding officer usually discouraged others from feeling the need to strike up a conversation. It was an inherent intimidation he'd gladly enjoy the benefits of that morning. His mind was already spinning with all the things that could go wrong. How they might fail.

Get Reynaldo killed.

All end up dead.

He glanced at the notes and maps on his com that detailed the site where Reynaldo was being held. Where he was caged like an animal. Remaining professional and not killing each human involved—one at a time, slowly and painfully—was going to require every ounce of self-control in Carl's arsenal.

Mixed species and pure-blooded big cats were still held captive all over the country, despite laws against it, but those poor prisoners didn't receive a full squad of soldiers to rescue them. Carl's influence and Rey's capture being part of the refugee camp breech helped rally forces around his recovery. In an hour, he'd be safe and free.

If not, Carl would no longer care about repercussions from slaughtering every human involved.

"We're almost there," the driver said. "Orders are to stop a quarter mile out so we have some element of surprise. They're more on guard at night, but a daytime raid has its own risks. There's not much cover. If they get wise, they might try to hide him or . . ."

He glanced nervously at Carl, but the general just nodded in response.

"Stay with that order," Carl said as calmly as he could. "The troops have a plan of attack to sneak in before the captors know what hit 'em."

The driver slowed to a stop, and Carl steeled himself before opening his door and facing the twelve armed soldiers climbing out of the back of the transport. Humid summer Mississippi air made it hard to breathe and wrapped smotheringly around him, a layer of sweat immediately coating his skin. A soldier handed the general the rest of his protective gear—a helmet with a radio and a flak jacket—as well as his weapon belt. After assuring all the laser guns were charged and ready, Carl nodded to the group and started off in the direction of the site.

The platoon captain—who was officially in charge of the team—used a scanner to check for security systems or booby traps. Hidden homemade explosives, like pipe bombs, were hard to spot. Backwoods humans tended to heavily protect their fortresses. Intel showed only three or four humans at the compound, but they would have the safety of cover. And the intel could be wrong. If they were prepared to stand their ground and demand their "rights" to keep the panthran, the operation could go off the rails quickly. When you entered battle against people who didn't give a shit about the rules or laws or the rights of living creatures, anything might happen. Lunatics were impossible to second-guess.

The platoon headed out at a quick pace through the thick air and tallgrass of the field, cicadas humming in the trees nearby. Within a few minutes of walking, the captain made a quick waving motion with his hand, and the team branched out in pairs, leaving the captain with Carl and two soldiers. One of them spun around to watch their backs, laser rifle at the ready, and the other took over the lead while the captain joined Carl.

Without a word, the captain held up his com and showed the general a photo of the compound ahead. He tapped one image: the shed where they believed Reynaldo was being held. It was well-hidden—how the kidnappers had managed to keep him for so long without being caught. Until that ex-girlfriend was thrilled to bring the law down on the head of the "rat bastard son-of-a-bitch" who'd cheated on her.

The lead soldier made a sharp noise through her teeth and stopped. The other three froze as well. Looking back at the captain, she pointed at her eye and then in the direction they were headed. She'd spotted the first outbuilding. The four crouched down in the tallgrass and waited for the signal that the other teams were in place and ready.

Not for the first time in his life, Carl wished he had panthran senses. Even from that distance, a feline-species creature would have been able to smell Reynaldo and positively zero in on his location. *Should have brought a tigran with us.*

Birds chirped in the trees. A dog barked in the distance. Carl glanced at the sparse woods around them. It was a lovely part of the country. Too bad he'd never be able to think about it now without rage burning in his throat.

The captain's radio light flashed green. The lead soldier rolled her head and shoulders, then aimed her rifle and started a low run through the waist-high grass. The other three spread out, watching for any sign of trap or defense. Nothing had shown on the scans, but low-tech devices could be just as damaging as the high-tech ones.

Up ahead, four large, gray metal storage buildings and the smaller one in the middle that reportedly held Reynaldo stood silent. The larger ones could hold a ptero-dragon like the four missing from the refugee camp raid. Carl hoped they'd get that lucky.

Shouts came from up ahead.

An explosion blasted fire into the air from the right side of the compound and shook the ground. Another came from somewhere at the back Carl couldn't see clearly.

Laser fire flashed from the woods, followed by several more from the other side of the compound. He ran flat-out, but the other three outpaced him, guns aimed ahead.

The door of one of the larger buildings flew open. An armed man wearing dark camo and a red baseball hat ran out in a blaze of gunfire. Return fire came from both sides, and the man was hit in the leg. He staggered into the small building and slammed the door behind him.

Carl froze, his gun hanging limply at his side, while the rest of the team converged on the compound. They hadn't gotten a jump on the captors. Maybe the men had been warned and were watching for an attack. Maybe there were cameras the Army hadn't spotted.

Whatever the reason, a desperate, injured man with a gun was now in with Reynaldo. Standard beginning of a hostage situation.

Carl watched the team secure the rest of the compound. Men in camo being led away from the buildings with their hands on their heads. The captain returned to where Carl was still standing.

"We have a complication, sir," he said, frowning.

"What's your plan?"

The captain tilted his head, probably knowing full well that Carl understood every option of the situation: storm the building, send a couple of troops in, or negotiate. Leaving was a possibility, but not a serious one. Carl would have to make the call. Ultimately, this was his mission. And he wasn't leaving without Rey.

"If we attack full-on," Carl said, "he's sure to kill Reynaldo. Just out of spite."

"Seems likely," the captain agreed.

"So, we try to negotiate."

"Or at least use that to distract him. There's a window in the back. If someone can get a shot from there, we could take him out."

Carl nodded and headed toward the small building, where most of the troops were now gathered, guns ready. Not one of them flinched as Carl and the captain walked to the front. Carl stood as tall and confident as he could, knowing the troops would respond to any reaction from inside the building. He just hoped it was before a shot hit him.

"This is General Carl Thompson of the United States Army," he called out. "It's over. Put your weapon down. Come out with your hands in the air."

There was no response.

"Don't make things worse than they are," Carl said. "Right now, your only crime is the kidnapping and holding of a mixed-species creature. If someone gets hurt . . . well, then you're into a whole mess of trouble. Years in jail, if not the rest of your life."

"Fuck off!" a muted male voice called from the building. "I'll blast a hole in his head if one of you comes closer!"

Carl choked back the fury and panic in his chest. "What would that accomplish?" he said as flippantly as he could. "Then we'll just light up the building."

The door opened a crack. "I know who you are, General *Freakfucker*. I watch the news. And I know what this abomination of nature means to you. Disgusting fuckers, both of you. You're not gonna let me kill him, though it'd be a blessing to the world. Both of you can go straight to hell!"

Carl's brain spun. This was suddenly about more than just holding on to a unique creature. There had been news interviews once the war was over, but he'd certainly never said anything about being mates. Same-sex and different-species relationships, while no longer illegal, were still "frowned upon" by many. It never occurred to Carl that searching so diligently for the panthran would reveal the truth and incite a bigot.

Before Carl could respond, the captain grabbed his arm firmly and stepped forward, blocking him from the line of fire.

"Let us see the panthran," the captain said. "For all we know, you're in there alone."

"I'm not letting that fucking demon out of his cage. I like my head attached to my body."

A flash of pride almost made Carl smile. Clearly, Reynaldo had demonstrated what he was capable of.

The captain turned and made eye contact with Carl. The general gave a small nod. *Do it.*

The captain made a flicking motion with his hand.

Soldiers rushed the door from both sides. In his heart, Carl knew it was the best strategy. This guy was never going to just come out and surrender. The longer they waited, the more desperate he'd become. If they could get someone inside, that was a step closer. Three soldiers were quickly in the building. Shouts and muffled threats carried outside. Carl stalked in, heart racing.

What he found was as bad as his nightmares. The 15-x-15-square-foot building was dank and dark, with only slight light from a small window at the far end that allowed some air in. Half of the room was a metal cage with a cot and a toilet. Nothing else. Like Reynaldo had been thrown back into his original disgusting home at the facility. But totally alone this time.

The emaciated panthran was hunkered down in a far corner. There was no glow from his golden eyes or movement, so it was impossible to tell if he was conscious. Or alive. The captor stood at the far end of the room, his gun aimed at Rey.

Nobody moved or spoke, but the ragged breathing of the injured man filled the room. Carl added "crazy eyes" to a worrying assessment of the man based on his clothing: green military-style camo pants and shirt, big work boots, and a red "Kerkaw Rules" baseball cap.

Carl holstered his gun—there were several others aimed at the man already—and showed his empty hands. The captor frowned but didn't lower his weapon. Carl hadn't expected him to.

"What's your name?" Carl asked the man.

"Fuck you!"

"No need for that," Carl said calmly. "Things still

haven't gotten too out of hand. No one's dead. We can all just walk out of here."

"Buck's dead! I saw him out there in the grass. You fuckers killed him!"

Remarks about deserving it and some nasty words of his own flitted through Carl's mind. Instead, he sighed. "That is an unfortunate loss. We'd hoped to remove this panthran from illegal captivity without any bloodshed."

The man snorted his disbelief. "Put down your guns, or I got nothin' to lose. I'll kill him. I swear I will."

Carl motioned for the troops to lower their weapons, which they did, setting them on the ground. Of course, he knew each of them had another gun on them somewhere, but he still hoped he could talk the man down.

Reynaldo hadn't moved or made a sound. The room reeked, but more of body odor and stale air than death or decay.

Seeming to sense the shift of the general's focus from him to the panthran, the man aimed the gun at Carl instead. Carl raised his hands slightly in front of him.

"I'd probably have time to kill you and the beast before one of you could get to me," the man said with a sneer. "Two homo fuckers down."

One of the female soldiers gave Carl a sideways glance, maybe checking for reaction. He wasn't going to be forced into showing his anger.

"That would be just a drop in the bucket," Carl said. "Still plenty of us to go around."

Rage bloomed in the man's eyes, and Carl realized

they had the key to it all. It may not have started out that way when Reynaldo was taken from the refugee camp, but this kidnapper had an agenda. The troops sensed it too, and Carl felt their readiness in the air. Not much longer before the man took a shot.

Reynaldo shifted and moaned. It was the tiniest bit of distraction, but it was enough. Instinctively, everyone turned to look at the panthran, including the kidnapper. There was a *schwep* and a flash of light, followed by the clunk of the kidnapper's gun as it hit the concrete floor. The man collapsed in a heap.

Two of the soldiers rushed forward, securing the man. Carl looked in the direction of the gunfire: the window. The soldier outside saluted, and Carl nodded in thanks.

Then he pulled off his helmet and rushed to the bars closest to Reynaldo, kneeling down to be eye level.

"Rey? I'm here. It's over now. We'll have you out in a second."

A pair of dark-golden eyes shone back at him.

"Carl? Is it really you?"

He reached through the bars, and Reynaldo crawled over, curling himself into his arms. The stench from his partner confirmed Carl's worst suspicions that the panthran had been caged and neglected. He could feel Reynaldo's ribs along his scarred back. The pair looked over at where the man lay, eyes open but unmoving. A brown scorch mark surrounded a hole from the laser blast on his forehead.

"Nice shot," the captain said, confirming the scene was locked down.

Carl vacillated between anger that the man was dead and couldn't suffer more and gratitude that they'd never have to listen to his hatefulness again.

"Good riddance," Reynaldo whispered.

One of the soldiers checked the man's pockets and came up with a digital key, then quickly opened the cage. She stepped in, followed by two other soldiers, prepared to help Reynaldo when he was ready. Rey looked up at them and smiled. Carl leaned his head against the panthran's through the bars. The kisses he longed to shower on his face would have to wait.

"Let's get you out of here," he said.

The soldiers helped Reynaldo stand and supported him to the door, where Carl met them. He wrapped a strong arm around Rey's waist and led him out the door of the building, just like he'd done years ago when they'd first met.

Once they were standing in the fresh air and green grass, Reynaldo sighed and relaxed. "I haven't seen the sky in forever."

The team moved away to give the pair some privacy and secure any evidence.

"I knew you'd find me," Reynaldo said, leaning his head on Carl's shoulder. "I never doubted it. I just hoped I'd still be alive when that day came."

"You can tell me all about it once we get home."

"It's a long way back to the camp."

"What? No." Carl realized Reynaldo probably had no idea what had happened in the world since he was taken. "The war's over, Rey. It ended just a few weeks after you were captured. We won. President Kerkaw ran off and is in hiding."

The panthran sighed again in deep relief. "They said they were doing Kerkaw's work and keeping me away from decent people."

Carl hugged him closer to his side. "No. They were just being shitheads. Dangerous shitheads. It's all over. Tigran and panthran and all the others are free."

"Free." Reynaldo flared his whiskers and inhaled the humid but fresh air. "So . . ." He turned to Carl. "If there's no camp, what happens now?"

"I'm sure they'll have some questions for you, to help the lawyers, then we go home."

"I don't have a home," Reynaldo said with a frown.

"Of course you do. My home. *Our* home. It's been waiting for you for two years."

"But . . . I can't live with you." The panthran glanced nervously around at the other soldiers.

"Everything's changed. Laws have changed."

Realizing they weren't fooling anyone there that day, Carl held him by the sides of the face and kissed him, right in front of everyone. It was quick and didn't come close to what he had planned for later, but it sent a message he'd no longer shy away from.

Reynaldo wiped tears from his deep-golden eyes and smiled at his mate.

"Okay, then. Home. Yeah, let's go home."

Legally
Wed

CHAPTER 1
JUNE 20, 2176

"You and Papa need to have a wedding like that," Aliania said, calling to her mother in the kitchen. "Dressed-up elephants and a party with dancing."

Taliya stopped trimming the venison roast for dinner and focused on the media wall. Ali had reached the end of the ancient Bollywood film *Bride and Prejudice*, where a big double wedding takes place. It was the epitome of a posh, luxurious Indian celebration, including gorgeous clothing, expensive jewelry sets, and the whole town singing and dancing. She smiled at her daughter. "You're not supposed to ride elephants like that now. They don't like it."

Ali kicked her feet thoughtfully along the back of the sofa. She'd been watching upside down, with her legs over the back of the couch and her head hanging where they should be.

"Okay," she agreed. "No elephants. But still a big wedding and a party."

"Wed-ding! Wed-ding! Wed-ding!" Amrita chanted from her chair at the kitchen table, where she'd been watching the movie and munching on jerky Grampa Jai had brought by earlier—the results of a weekend of hunting and deer processing.

"Par-ty! Par-ty! Par-ty!" Little Jai shouted over her, trying to sneak a strip of steak off the counter.

Taliya smacked at his hand. "Not raw," she cautioned. "Remember, bugs and disease."

Little Jai squinched his face and rushed over to snag some jerky from his almost-three-year-old twin sister instead, who protested with a loud screech. Taliya added the venison and some seasoning to the veggies already prepped in a slow-roasting pot and set it to cook for dinner.

Ali rolled off the sofa and met her at the sink. "We could have the wedding here," the pure-white kit suggested, her blue eyes sparkling and crossing a bit with excitement. "Samson would officiatate it this time too, I bet."

"Officiate." Taliya chuckled as she dried her hands. "And you're just looking for an excuse to have Samson come visit."

Little Jai hooted a laugh and made kissy noises. Ali stuck her tongue out at him. Her brother tossed jerky at her, which she caught with a chomp and chewed while looking like she was pondering a new front of ideas.

"It wouldn't have to be an Indian-style wedding." Ali flopped across the back of the sofa to grab her com and said into it, "Show me a fancy wedding."

A dozen images appeared in boxes on the media wall, all of them human ceremonies.

"That's a lot of expensive-looking options," Taliya said, coming to stand behind the sofa.

Ali clicked on one image, and what must have been a royal wedding displayed in video. A massive old church, more flowers than were logical, and the bride in a voluminous pile of white satin with puffy sleeves and a train dragging twenty yards behind her.

"Is there actually a woman under there somewhere?" Taliya said.

"Okay," Ali admitted, "not like *that.*"

Taliya put her hand on Ali's back as she tilted precariously, worried the kit would fall forward and whack her head on the coffee table. Again. "Definitely not like that."

"But you should do *something,*" Ali said, finishing her flop over the back onto the sofa and sprawling out. "Some kind of wedding."

At almost six now, Taliya understood Ali's newfound fascination with relationships and weddings and all that, but she and Kano were content with their handfasting from the first day at the refugee camp and all it had symbolized. In the moment, it might have been out of necessity, but they'd long ago agreed that their future was together, forever.

"Don't you want to marry Papa?"

Taliya shifted her gaze from the ridiculous wedding on the wall to her daughter, who genuinely looked concerned. "We're already married, kitten. You may not remember, but you were there."

"I *don't* remember." Ali frowned. "And that stuff at the camp wasn't really a wedding. It wasn't *legal*. But it can be now."

That point was true. Part of Samson's work with the government had been allowing creatures to become legally married again—with all the rights and privileges that came with it, just like humans.

"When Papa comes home, we should have a real wedding."

Taliya leaned on the back of the sofa, closer to the kit. "Why's that so important to you?"

Glancing back at the media wall, Ali said, "It's what grown-ups are supposed to do when they live together and have families. Now that tigran can do it again too..."

"You think we should just because we can?"

Ali shrugged one shoulder. "Samson says it proves that we creatures are civilized and do want those rights. Every pair who gets married will show the world we're not animals."

"Oh." Taliya pursed her whiskers, and the tip of her tail flicked. Samson had said those things on a video call last week, but she hadn't realized Ali was paying attention. Which was dumb because if Samson was talking, Ali was always paying attention. "I tell you what. When Papa gets back tomorrow, you can talk to him about it."

"He'll want to marry you," Ali said with confidence. She rolled off the sofa and came around to give Taliya a hug. "I know he will."

Taliya squeezed her—noting that the kit's head was now almost up to her chin—and gave her a kiss on the top of her head. "I don't doubt it for a moment."

After they'd discussed the potential wedding, Little Jai broke something in his room, and Amrita gagged on some jerky. Taliya didn't think about it again in the fluster of daily life and collapsed into bed as soon as the kits were asleep. She neglected to warn Kano.

⸺⬥⸻

THE NEXT AFTERNOON, THE GUARD DOGS—BELGIAN MALINOIS Cairo and Elektra—barked that over-the-moon, almost howl they did when their favorite male in the world returned home. He'd been gone two weeks this time, working on the construction of levies around Baton Rouge. The sound of a small transport pulling up to the house confirmed Kano's return.

"Papaaa!" Ali screamed as she thundered down the hall from her bedroom and straight out the front door.

Amrita and Little Jai were next door, hanging out with their uncles Tuscan and Tyler, allowing Taliya some quiet time with a good book. She smiled and slipped a marker in to save her spot before greeting her mate.

From the doorway, she heard Aliania accost her father.

"Papa, you need to marry Mama. Mama says she'll

marry you. And I know you'll marry her. So we're gonna have a wedding."

Kano glanced up at Taliya on the porch, black lines on his forehead drawn down in confusion. He still had one foot in the transport with the dogs sniffing his shoes and wriggling around him. "A wedding?"

"Yep, a wedding." Ali dragged him out of the car and hugged him around the middle. "Right away."

Taliya hoped the kit remembered she was too big now for her father to carry as Ali looked ready to climb into Kano's arms.

The familiar human driver smiled at Kano as he handed over his luggage. "Good luck, man."

Ali trailed on her father's heels, the dogs racing around them, while he carried the bags up onto the porch and the transport gave a quick farewell honk.

"Welcome home," Taliya said with a slow-blink.

Kano set down the bags and pulled her in for an embrace, the scents of Louisiana bayous and exhaustion thick in his fur. "*Who's* getting married?" he mumbled into her ear.

"Your daughter has decided that we are."

He pulled back and turned to Ali, hovering inches from them. "I see."

"It's legal again," Ali said assuredly. "Samson said so. And he knows everything. So you need to get married now."

Taliya chuffed at the girl. "Give Papa a few minutes to settle in, then we can talk about it."

Aliania narrowed her eyes suspiciously but nodded. Patience was not one of her strongest qualities, and she'd been holding on to it for almost twenty-four hours since the determination to see them legally wed had seized her. Taliya had expected it was just the Ali-thing du jour, but apparently not.

"Go get the twins." Taliya picked up one of Kano's bags. "Tell them Papa's home."

They watched as the kit stomped her way across the yard, dogs at her heels, to retrieve her siblings.

"It always feels like I missed a hundred things while I'm away," Kano said, tail swishing.

Taliya carried a bag inside and left it next to the laundry machines. "This just started yesterday. I forgot all about it."

"Our daughter obviously did not."

Kano set his other bag down and unzipped the side. Dank odors of rot and putridness burst out. Taliya covered her nose with a whuff. He scooped most of the tunics and slacks into the washer, setting aside heavier work pants and shirts for the next load.

Taliya pinched his work boots out and held them at arm's length. "These go outside."

"Nothing like the unique smell of the swamp," he said, squinching his nose. "I'll deal with them later."

The squeals of the kits returning from their grandparents came through the open door, but they all stopped at the entrance and covered their faces. "Eeewww!"

"Should have opened the bags outside." Kano chuckled.

"Papa," Ali said, putting her hands on her hips, "you will have to deal with this stink before we can even consider hosting a wedding."

⸺⸙⸺

BECAUSE KANO WAS HOME, THE WHOLE FAMILY GATHERED FOR dinner that night in the main house, including Aunty Marla and her orange-and-black tigran husband Parth. Summer rain plinked off the windows, with the occasional roll of thunder vibrating the floor. Vegetables from the garden, a haunch of roasted venison, and Aunty Marla's nutty wheat bread were passed around the large kitchen table.

Shreya confirmed everyone was served before sitting down and grinning at Taliya. "So, Ali tells me there's going to be a wedding as soon as possible."

The table went silent, and everyone looked back and forth between Shreya and her daughter. Aliania giggled. Amrita and Jai began their banging chants.

"Wed-ding! Wed-ding!"

"Par-ty! Par-ty!"

Tuscan and Tyler joined in, but Taliya suspected more to make noise than encourage matrimonial plans. At nearly ten years old, her twin brothers were eking their way out of the human teen-style years. Taller than her, but still gangly and acting like kits as much as they could get away with. She regretted letting her own twins sit across the table with her rowdy brothers.

"Okay, okay," Kano said, shooting a stern glance at each of the offenders until they settled back into eating—but smiling and moving like they were still chanting in their heads.

Marla cut a slice of bread and handed it to Grampa Jai beside her. "You two are going to have a wedding? Like, the whole formal thing?"

Taliya bristled her whiskers. "It's Ali's latest obsession."

"Mama." Ali huffed. "It's not an *obsession*. But I'm not going to stop talking about it until you do it."

"Kitten, I believe that's the definition of obsession."

Aliania popped a bite of meat into her mouth and shrugged one shoulder.

"We could do something simple," Marla said. "Is it the legally married part that's important to you, Ali? Or the big celebration part?"

"Both."

Kano set his fork down. "We are not having hundreds of humans over to dance on the lawn or elephants or any of the stuff you saw in that movie."

"Oh, I know *that*." Aliania rolled her blue eyes. "But it could be all of us and Samson and Uncle Carl and Reynaldo too. You can't have a wedding without a party."

Taliya met Marla's gaze, and they shared a slow-blink. Parth frowned but didn't comment further. The pair were legally married in Canada, but it had been the briefest of exchanged vows. Necessary paperwork before they left the refugee camp a year after the war ended and came to live in Arkansas near Taliya and her family. More of a technicality to ensure their safety and partnership out in the world than anything romantic. It had never occurred to Taliya to hold some kind of celebration. In her lifetime, tigran couldn't get married. Maybe it was time to reinstitute some joyful traditions.

"If we keep it to just those creatures," Taliya said, "it could be fun." She looked to Kano, and he smiled and nodded.

"And Uncle Carl," Ali said firmly.

"What?"

"Uncle Carl is not a creature." Ali pursed her lips, like she was expecting to be challenged.

Taliya chuckled. "No, I suppose he's not. I forget that sometimes."

"He growls like a creature," Amrita said. "And can find me during hide-and-seek as well as the dogs."

Aliania grinned. "That's just because you're a terrible hider."

The girls tossed bits of bread at each other until Shreya cleared her throat loudly to remind them of basic table manners. Taliya's pointed glare had managed to keep Little Jai and her brothers from joining in.

"It was the first legal right we lost," Grampa Jai said, redirecting the conversation, "when Kerkaw set his sights on tigran. No more marriages of creatures."

Since the war ended, Taliya's life had been wrapped

up in fighting for tigran rights to be restored. It did seem logical to celebrate this specific victory.

"Will I walk you down an aisle and give you away?" Grampa Jai asked, buttering a slice of bread. "Or going more Indian tradition?"

Kano rumbled a laugh. "It seems a bit late to hand your daughter over to me." He glanced at the twins. "That's some fur shed long ago."

"No virginal veil to be symbolically lifted, then?" Shreya smirked.

Tuscan and Tyler both made gagging noises and grabbed their throats, egging each other on to more exaggeration of their disgust. The kits looked confused, wondering what their uncles were on about.

"A *simple* wedding," Taliya said firmly, meeting Ali's gaze and hopefully changing the subject. "And a party with close friends and family. I'll agree to that."

Ali pursed her whiskers, considering the proposition. "Fine. But you're missing a step. Papa has to propose."

Kano stood dramatically, the scrape of his chair making everyone at the table turn his way. With long strides and marching arms, he sauntered over to Taliya, turned her and her chair to face him, and dropped to one knee. Taking her hand amid the laughter of the family, he placed his other hand on his heart.

"Taliya, my dearest love and the mother of my offspring . . ."

Tuscan and Tyler resumed gagging, and Shreya shushed them.

Kano continued, undeterred. "Will you do me the honor of becoming my wife, even though we've been married for years now? It will make our eldest happy."

"Yes, of course." Taliya chuffed and squeezed his hand. "I will marry you officially."

A cheer went up from the table, with Aliania the loudest. She stood on her chair and did a wiggle dance. Little Jai, Amrita, Tuscan, and Tyler resumed their chanting of wedding and party. Kano stood, kissed Taliya on the forehead, helped Ali sit back down before she fell, and returned to his seat.

"We keep it *simple*," Kano said, looking pointedly at Ali.

"Whatever you say, Papa."

"I'll call Samson and Carl to see what works with their schedules," Taliya said.

Amrita climbed into Taliya's lap and poked her cheek to get her full attention. "Be sure to invite Reynaldo. I want to meet him. I don't remember him from before. Just Uncle Carl's stories."

"I will." Taliya squeezed the kit, adoring her gentle heart. "Rey might not be ready to attend an event away from home just yet, but I'll make sure he knows we'd love to have him come too."

Taliya met Kano's eye, and he smiled sadly. They hadn't seen Reynaldo in person since he was recovered from the kidnappers. She hoped he felt up to coming so she could put hands on him and assure herself he was safe after so many months and so much worry.

"Next we have to decide what to wear," Ali said. "It can't just be normal stuff."

Marla cut some meat for Little Jai and nodded thoughtfully. "Sounds like Diwali clothes are coming out of the attic."

Taliya started to say that was too much bother, and the look on Kano's face suggested he was ready to shut that down and avoid the hassle. But it was a relatively easy solution to meeting Ali's wedding agenda. "That sounds like a great idea."

"I wonder if mine from last year still fits." Aliania giggled, bopped in her seat, and sing-songed, "I may need something new."

Taliya huffed. "We'd best get this done quickly before things spiral and elephants somehow get involved."

Tuscan blasted a serviceable elephant trumpet and jumped up to stomp around the room, pretending his arm was a trunk. Amrita climbed on his back and began finger-tutting and bouncing her shoulders. Tyler and Little Jai clapped a rhythm for her to follow.

"Painted elephants wearing costumes," Ali said with a grin, standing to join her sister's dance.

Shreya chuckled. "Oh dear. Gods protect us."

⸻⋄⋄⋄⸻

ONCE DINNER AND CLEANUP WAS DONE, THE OTHERS RETURNED to their homes and Taliya gathered her kits to call Washington, D.C. She'd sent messages and arranged for a group video chat but hadn't told them what it was about. Aliania couldn't sit still, anticipating her adored "uncles" on the media wall.

Taliya started the calls, and moments later Carl and Reynaldo appeared on half of the wall, both in casual tunics and slacks for an evening at home. The pair sat on a dark-brown sofa in the middle of their tidy living room in military quarters—active duty for General Carl Thompson still in play, though mostly political intrigue now since the war was over.

Rey looked nervous but more like she remembered him from their time together at camp as dragon wranglers. It had only been two weeks since Carl was finally able to rescue his mate from the kidnappers who'd held him prisoner for over two years. They'd video chatted with Taliya not long after that, and she'd been horrified by how thin and exhausted Rey looked. Not at all the confident, magnificent panthran who'd turned heads of humans and creatures alike. Taliya sighed and slow-blinked at him, grateful to see healing and recovery were moving forward. Emotional scars were impossible to see. Time would hopefully help with those as well, though Taliya often wondered how Reynaldo functioned at all with the abuse his life had involved.

"Uncle Carl!" all three kits screamed, rushing up to the wall like he was really right there.

Carl leaned forward and pretended to bop both girls on the head. "Hello, my little marshmallow. And my strawberry sundae." Shifting to a stern expression, he gave a salute. "Private Rama."

Little Jai jumped to attention stiffly and returned the salute. "General Thompson."

"At ease, soldier." Carl grinned and put a hand on Reynaldo's knee.

The kits clambered onto the sofa, and Ali all but hovered over the cushion between her parents, excitement wafting from her in waves.

"Guess what!" she gushed.

Kano steadied her and smiled. "Hold on. Wait for Samson."

The other half of the wall image was already coming into focus on the legal office where Samson the ligran spent most of his waking hours. It was beige and brown around him, and the creature was settling into an armchair instead of behind his desk. He smiled and waved as the full connection completed. He, too, was in comfortable slacks and a tunic instead of a business suit, which always looked out of place on the eight foot creature.

Aliania wiggled at the sight of him. Taliya and Kano exchanged side-eye grins. Their daughter was at such an odd age. Tall now, but still gawky and young. Rather like a Great Dane puppy or a baby giraffe.

"Good evening," Samson said. "Carl and Rey, good to see you as well. Are we still on for the deposition tomorrow morning?"

The pair nodded somberly, and Taliya's stomach clenched. Samson was handling the prosecution against

Reynaldo's kidnappers, though it would probably take months for any kind of justice.

"No. Talking. About. Work!" Ali said, bouncing with each word.

The three males on the media wall looked back toward her and smiled.

"Sorry, little one," Samson said.

Taliya steadied her daughter again and said, "Aliania has some news and an invitation for you."

"Wedding!" the kit squealed.

"Wed-ding! Wed-ding!" Amrita and Little Jai chanted and clapped before Kano and Taliya calmed all three of them down. Ali bobbed so excitedly, Kano set her on the ground before she fell off the sofa. She sat crisscross, but her knees bounced.

Carl, Reynaldo, and Samson just looked confused.

"You are hosting a wedding?" Samson asked in his deep, resonant voice.

"Yes! Mama and Papa are getting married," Ali announced, seeming a bit annoyed that the males didn't understand immediately.

The trio on the media wall stared blankly for a second before Carl asked, "Again?"

"Ali does not feel," Taliya explained, "that we are officially and legally married. So we would like to invite you to join us for a wedding ceremony here on the property."

Aliania nodded her approval of this information. "And Samson must . . ." She frowned for a second. "O-ffi-ci-ate."

"I would be honored." Samson smiled. "Creatures

becoming legally married is actually very important right now."

"I know!" Ali said, leaping up and standing inches from his image on the wall. "You said so last week!"

Samson tipped his head at the kit. "Yes, I did. You are very observant, Miss Aliania."

Delighted chortles and rumbles came from Ali. "That's when I decided that Mama and Papa needed to get married."

"Yes," Kano said, "this is all your fault, Samson."

He chuckled and slow-blinked. "I take full responsibility."

Taliya noticed Carl and Rey whispering to each other. "You three have a lot going on, but we wanted to make sure you were invited if it's possible to get away for a couple of days."

Carl kept a hand firmly on Rey's knee as he asked, "Do you have a date in mind?"

"June twenty-seventh," Ali shouted. "Mama's birthday!"

Everyone froze for a second, and Kano let out a whuff. "But kitten," he said, "that's in five days."

"I know." Ali tucked herself in under Taliya's arm and cuddled close. "But that way it will be easy to remember the anniversary. And another reason for a party."

Taliya blinked twice to clear her thoughts and hugged Aliania. "I suppose it would. Not like we normally do big birthday parties."

"But it's your twenty-first birthday. Isn't that supposed to be one of those that's a big deal?"

Kano chuckled, as did Carl and Samson.

"That's a human thing," Taliya said, leaning back a bit to meet Ali's eyes. "You can legally buy alcohol when you're twenty-one. Tigran don't worry about that so much."

"You drink ale all the time," Ali said with a smirk.

Little Jai chimed in, "And we never buy it. Grampa makes it himself."

Taliya felt like the conversation was getting off track, but the males on the media wall looked very entertained. None of them had offspring yet.

"The twenty-seventh is a Thursday," Samson said. "A bit tricky for those of us with jobs. As long as you promise to provide lots of that ale, I'm sure it can all be arranged."

Taliya frowned. "Or it could just be on Saturday or Sunday."

"No!" Aliania insisted. "On your birthday. Done."

Kano met Taliya's gaze and shrugged. It was easier to agree than set up a battle of wills with Aliania. Taliya picked her battles routinely and still often admitted defeat.

"Thursday it is. And ale for everyone, I guess," Taliya said.

Taliya looked to Carl and Rey, who were whispering again. Even tigran ears couldn't pick up what their home media system didn't catch. Maybe they had it muted. "Carl, we understand if you can't get the day off. Or if it's too soon for making the trip and being in a big group, but we would love it if you could join us."

Carl turned back toward the camera and smiled. "Wouldn't miss it. We're just remembering, we were both there for the handfasting."

"You were?"

Rey nodded with a slight smile. "We stood side by side and listened to your vows." He flared his dark whiskers. "That was the day Carl came back into my life."

The couple exchanged loving smiles, and Taliya blew out a breath. They'd been to hell and back since that day. She hoped the future was bright for them now.

"And we'll be there for this wedding too," Carl said. "Tell us when, and we'll figure it out."

Aliania huffed. "I told you when. Thursday, on Mama's birthday."

"If it stays small and simple," Taliya said, pulling a squirmy Amrita onto her lap. "We can manage that."

Samson grabbed his com and started tapping away. "It is a deal. I will make travel arrangements for the three of us from D.C."

Carl gave a lazy salute, probably thrilled for someone else to handle the complicated details of getting them to Arkansas. Samson and Rey couldn't just hop on a commercial plane. The government or military usually got involved.

"You can stay over at the grandparents' house," Kano said as Little Jai hung over his back and jumped happily on the sofa cushions. "The T-twins can set up a dome in the yard."

"Hopefully, we can arrive Wednesday afternoon," Samson said, looking up from his com, "so we will see you then. And congratulations."

Taliya's skin tingled at how soon that was, but it did meet her goal of moving quickly before details got out of hand. "Thanks. See you then!"

She disconnected the call, and all three kits jumped off the sofa to dance around the living room in celebration.

Kano reached over and pulled her in under his arm. "I guess it's settled then."

"But . . ." Taliya snuggled in tighter. "You leave again two days after. No honeymoon. Married folks are supposed to get a honeymoon vacation."

"My whole life with you is a honeymoon." Kano kissed the top of her head.

She chuckled as the kits strutted past in a conga line of victory. "Sweet sentiment, but not a vacation."

"We'll plan something for later."

"Guess I should talk to Marla about a cake. That's what you do, right?"

"Cake! Cake! Cake!" Amrita started the chant, and her siblings joined in.

⚜

THE NEXT AFTERNOON, THE DOGS BARKING ALERTED TALIYA TO A

stranger on the property. Kano staggered through the front door carrying a crate almost as large as him.

"This was just delivered by a special courier." He set it on the huge family meal table and put his hands on his hips. "The label says it's from the president."

"From Padme?" Taliya stopped folding laundry and joined him in the kitchen.

All three kits had followed him in and gathered around. A card attached to the package said: *Congratulations on your wedding. Love, P.* Samson must have shared the news of the upcoming nuptials.

"That's a big present," Taliya said, touched the president had moved so quickly to get something for them. Lifting the lid from the bamboo shipping crate, her breath caught in her throat.

Aliania gasped and grabbed Taliya's arm. "Oh, Mama ..."

"Well," Kano said. "I'm gonna need something fancier now."

Padme couldn't have special ordered the wedding sari lying in that box, so it must have been hastily tailored from a glorious human outfit. Pulling back the tissue, Taliya lifted the top portion to see it better.

The silky fabric was a deep forest-green, with two-inch gold trim covered in sparkles and spangles that glinted in the light. Elaborate black embroidery ran through the bordering, making it even more extravagant. The skirt was similar fabric, including a gold band of trim at the bottom. The dupatta—traditionally worn over the head like a veil at weddings—was sheer black with edging in matching green and gold. Taliya had never seen a more beautiful piece of clothing in real life, and Padme had taken her to a dozen fancy events over the years, providing some lovely saris. It was even green instead of the more wedding-traditional red, which Taliya felt clashed with her orange fur.

"It's perfect."

"Try it on," Amrita whispered, like the moment was too magical to disturb.

Taliya whuffed. "Feels like I should shower first."

Reaching in to gently touch the silk, Ali chortled. "I need a dress that matches."

"Me too," Amrita said.

Jai snorted. "Not me. I like my Diwali outfit."

Kano sighed, pulled out his com like he was going to type a message, then just said, "Little Jai, go get Grandma. We've got three days to match the elegance of this presidential sari."

<hr>

By the time she headed back home for dinner, Shreya had a plan for dresses in a lighter shade of green with black and gold trim for Amrita and Aliania. Measurements were taken of the enthusiastic, giggly kits. Fabric remnants would make a tie to add to Kano's suit, which was fortunately black and already matched the wedding outfit from Padme. He'd only worn it once, for a political event he'd attended with Taliya. Shreya promised she could find or create clothing for the rest of the family that would be dressy and coordinate with the sari. After a trip to town in the morning, she'd report back on the fabric options.

Aunty Marla had stopped by during the process and agreed to change her matron of honor ensemble to a two-piece black, shimmery outfit Taliya had worn to a United Nations dinner. Shreya noted a few necessary alterations and added it to the sewing list that Taliya suspected would keep her mother busy nonstop until the ceremony.

Taliya had watched the process with delight and awe at her mother and how she managed to sew, regardless of her declawed hands. It wasn't a skill many humans still possessed, but Shreya had learned as part of her husband's research on early U.S. history. Once tigran no longer felt safe out in the world, it was a highly useful talent. She'd made the family's clothes for years, though now they tended to trade for items instead. Shreya seemed thrilled with the project, making all kinds of notes and sketches of her plans.

After the kits were in bed and she'd showered, Taliya pulled the crate from the closet, where she'd hidden it to keep her young from accidentally destroying the sari. Trying it on carefully, she found the ensemble fit perfectly. A thrill spiked her hackles as she pulled the dupatta over the top of her head. Taliya didn't think of herself as vain, but imagining the upcoming wedding and wearing this outfit—

"No!" she yelled at the first click of the bedroom door opening.

It stopped moving. "Everything okay?" Kano said from the other side.

"I have the sari on," she admitted. "I don't want you to see."

He chuckled. "How very civilized of you."

"It's not any silly superstition." She glanced back in the mirror, startled by how fantastic she looked. "I just want it to be a surprise."

Kano was quiet for a moment. Then he whispered through the crack in the door, "Okay. But don't bother putting your PJs on after it's hidden away again."

Smiling as she turned sideways to admire the outfit, she whispered back, "I'm sure that can be arranged."

CHAPTER 2

Shreya arrived home from her trip to town the next morning while Taliya and Aliania were still restoring the kitchen after breakfast. She carried two canvas bags of fabric and supplies over to the cleaned table and set them down, a worried expression tugging at the black lines of her face.

"Were you not able to find what you needed?" Taliya asked, drying her hands and joining her mother at the table.

"Oh, no. It's all fine. But I did something you may not like."

Taliya glanced at the bags, which appeared to contain all the important items and lovely light-green silky fabric. She couldn't imagine what had her normally poised mother so upset.

"Well," Shreya said, clutching her hands over her

stomach, "I may have mentioned what all of this was for in the presence of a couple of tigran."

"Did you invite them?" Ali said, closing up the dishwasher. "I hope so. I already invited my friends' families."

"What?" Shreya and Taliya both said, turning to the kit.

Aliania pursed her whiskers at them. "It can't just be family. That's not a party."

Taliya rolled her shoulders. "Okay, we'll get back to how many creatures you've added to the day in a moment. What happened at the store?"

"They asked so many questions," Shreya said. "I told them we were putting something simple together in a few days, but I could tell how excited they were. They wanted to celebrate too. So yes, I invited them."

Taliya inhaled deeply and blew it out. "So . . . you'll write down who you invited. And Ali, you'll do the same." Any tigran in the Ozarks counted as part of their far-flung community, mostly separated by the acres of land each family had for farming and hunting. "If it's spread this much, we have to include everyone. You know that, right?" She glanced back and forth between the two offenders, doing a mental count on who that guest list would include.

"Of course," Aliania said with a glint in her blue eyes, like maybe that had been the agenda all along.

"Kitten," Shreya said, putting her hand on Taliya's, "you're talking about over fifty tigran."

"And the family of cheeman who moved in last week," Ali said.

Taliya wiped a hand across her face. "I guess so. If we've opened the door to anyone in the community, it would be insulting to leave some families out."

Ali's shoulders bounced to some internal rhythm, and she started subtly finger-tutting a dance.

"But that's it," Taliya said firmly, which didn't dissuade the kit at all. "Don't put out some invitation to the world of creatures. Are we clear?"

"Crys-tal," Ali said with a grin. "Sixty guests is enough."

"Great gods." Shreya sighed and plopped down in a kitchen chair.

Ali danced around the kitchen, singing the big finale song from the film that started all of this drama. "'A marriage has come to town....'"

Taliya wondered if "town" was going to be happy about all of the tigran converging in one place nearby. Humans and tigran in this area went back a century, but tensions and fearful sentiments from the Gathering still hovered.

Taliya peeked through the bags and the piles of fabric. "Who's going to cook for all of these creatures if you have so much sewing to do?"

"Not you!" Aliania called out.

Taliya and Shreya exchanged smiles. Taliya's cooking skills had improved out of necessity, but her talents were still limited.

"Well, no," Taliya said. "Except the basics."

"We may need to do some trading," Shreya said. "That's a lot of creatures to feed. And we only have a few days."

Ali danced her way out the front door. "I'll get Papaaa," she sing-songed. "He can figure out the food."

Taliya sat next to her mother and looked around the house aimlessly, like she might find an answer on how to go back in time and say no to all of this.

"It will all be fine," Shreya said. "It's been years since we had a party for our community. It's time."

"I agree. Just wish it wasn't *me* at the center of it."

Kano stepped through the doorway with a dazed expression on his face. Outside, Aliania was dancing around the yard. He glanced back at her, then at Taliya and Shreya. "Why am I cooking a feast for sixty creatures?"

"Turns out," Taliya said, "your eldest already started inviting friends, and more neighbors found out when Mother was at the store. We have to include everyone."

Shreya shrugged her shoulders innocently. "It's not *all* my fault."

"All right." Kano shut the door and joined them at the table. His ears twisted back to front. "That's a lot of guests and a lot of food and I'm assuming ale too."

"Grampa Jai will clean out his stores for this wedding. You know he will." Taliya hesitated, a memory tickling the back of her mind. "Remember when he studied human celebrations and there was that part about making people bring food to the party instead of expecting it to be provided?"

Kano frowned. "That's a real thing?"

Shreya stood and opened the door. "Grampa Jai!"

"What is it, wife?" he called back from across the clearing. He and the T-twins were on their porch planning a song list for the party. Ali had already joined them.

"We have a human history question."

Taliya could see the spark in his eyes from yards away. Her father loved talking about human history and all its odd quirks. He hopped up and jogged over to join them at the main house.

"I am prepared to share all my *vast* knowledge on the subject," he said, leaning his stocky body against the kitchen island for a second to catch his breath. "What are we discussing?"

"The tradition of 'Come to my party, but bring your own meal,'" Kano said.

"Ah." Grampa Jai smiled. "BYOB."

Taliya tried to work the acronym out for some reference to food but came up short. Shreya and Kano looked like they were doing the same.

"Actually," Grampa Jai said, "that's more for alcoholic beverages, so the party can be big but the host doesn't have to spend a fortune paying for it. Bring your own booze. BYOB."

"I'm thinking we'll provide the ale," Shreya said. "But what about food? Taliya's remembering something about that."

Her father flexed his whiskers proudly. "Such a good student. Yes, bring your own food is different. It's called a 'potluck.' As in, you hope you get lucky and like what someone else brings for your guests to eat."

"So people just show up with food, and you get what you get?" Taliya imagined a whole table spread of nothing but mushy casseroles. Humans *loved* casseroles.

"Sometimes." Her father considered it. "I have seen evidence of requests being made for certain dishes or guests discussing the options and trying to plan. But usually the random 'luck' of it was considered part of the fun."

Kano huffed. "Dare we try it? That would certainly make planning easier. It's so last-minute, would our neighbors understand?"

"Actually," Shreya said, "I think it would be a lovely tradition to establish. About being able to offer your lair for a party without having to prepare dozens of dishes."

Taliya grinned. "If I threaten to cook, that would inspire them."

Her family laughed and nodded.

Kano said, "I'm not sure legends of your limited kitchen skills have gone out far and wide, but maybe some invitation that comes with the whole 'put together quickly' note and asking for a favorite celebratory food item to share."

"Perfect," Grampa Jai said. "Instead of 'help us, please,' it's about coming together as a community again. We've let that get away from us since the war."

Amrita and Little Jai thundered down the hall, giggling. They stopped in their tracks at the sight of both their parents and their grandparents in the kitchen.

"We didn't do it," Little Jai said with a serious expression.

"At least *I* didn't," Amrita said, nudging her twin brother with an elbow.

Taliya opened her arms with a smile. "Come here, you silly kittens." They raced over to climb in her lap. "We're just talking about food for the wedding. There are going to be a lot of guests now."

Amrita's golden-green eyes went wide at that. "Will they come in our house? In my room?"

"No, no. Nothing like that. It's just becoming a big party."

"To celebrate you and Papa getting married?" Amrita said, wrapping her tail around Taliya's leg.

"Yes."

Amrita grabbed her mother's hand in excitement. "Can Disha come?"

Disha was one tigran friend the kit seemed to favor, though they didn't get to see each other often since Amrita couldn't safely attend preschool in town. Taliya squeezed her daughter's hand. "Absolutely. With her whole family."

Little Jai had already wiggled down from Taliya's lap and was heading for the front door. Before he could open it, Aliania burst in.

"I know what the invitations should look like!" she

gushed before strutting to the sofa and falling over the back onto the cushions. "We can have them sent out in minutes."

Shreya stood and collected her supply bags. "That sounds very helpful, Aliania." She met Taliya's gaze and winked. "I'm sure your mother will appreciate the help."

Taliya slow-blinked and swallowed down what she was going to say about handling that herself. "How about we prepare them together, Ali? Then we can be sure all the important information is included." *And you don't offer up something bizarre.*

She couldn't see the kit's face, but Ali's foot hanging over the back of the sofa bounced thoughtfully. "Okay. I suppose."

"Because we'll need to explain the whole potluck thing," Grandpa Jai said.

Aliania's head popped up over the sofa. "A pot *what*?"

"You start with how you want the invitations to look," Kano said, moving over to her on the sofa, "and your mother and I will figure out what they need to say so everything's clear and goes out to the whole community at one time. Deal?"

The kit scrunched her nose but then nodded. "Fine. But they're going to be dark-green, like Mama's sari."

"That's a great idea." Taliya set Amrita to stand next to her and rested her palms on the kitchen table. "Okay. Here we go. Mother, you sew until you can't sew any more. Kano, figure out what the message will say. Father, make that playlist some serious dancing music. I'm going to . . . I don't even know." Taliya tiger moaned, wondering once again how she'd gotten roped into this drama.

The dryer buzzed the end of a cycle, and Shreya chuckled. "Start with getting that. Then you can figure out how to set up the lawn with tables and chairs. There's a shop in town where we can rent them. Plates and silverware too."

"Okay." Taliya sighed. "That should cover all of it, right?"

"It's June." Grampa Jai crossed his arms over his chest. "Are we seriously planning an assembly of tigran in the full sun of our yard? It could be a hundred degrees."

Ali huffed, like they were all making it complicated. "We need a canopy and some cool blowers. Easy."

"I'm sure we can rent those as well," Kano said. "And let's plan for evening. Maybe a little less scorching then. And makes it easier for anyone with a day job to attend."

Most tigran stuck to their own property and were self-sufficient, in general, or traded with local businesses. Kano and his masonic work was a rarity. A mid-week wedding shouldn't be an issue for many tigran, but later in the day was still a good idea.

Taliya made a list on her com and looked back at the group. "Anything else?"

"You know," Ali said, "there's still one thing missing to make it *perfect.*"

Her eyes twinkled as she glanced among the adults.

"No," Kano said. "No elephants."

WITHIN AN HOUR, INVITATIONS HAD BEEN SENT OUT OVER Taliya's com to every tigran in the Ozarks, the new cheeman family—whom Samson had helped relocate—and even a few humans, like the local shopkeepers, who'd known the family for years. The guest list now ran around eighty individuals.

Aliania designed a lovely dark-green background with gold lettering, so it met her standard of fanciness. They kept the text simple.

Thursday, June 27th, at 6:00 pm
Join Kano Rama and Taliya Sharma
to celebrate their official marriage ceremony.
As your gift for the couple,
please bring a favorite food item
to share with the community.

Taliya was grateful to accomplish the invites before word spread and anyone's fur was rumpled. When she'd called to rent the supplies and equipment, the owner of that business already knew about the event. Fortunately, he didn't seem to expect an invitation. They had to draw the line somewhere. She'd never even met the guy. The yard was big, but it was going to be crowded if everyone actually showed up.

The whole simple wedding cake idea wasn't going to

work with so many guests, and creatures, in general, didn't get overly excited about sweets. Instead, they decided to leave it to the luck of the food contributions. Marla would tip the scales by making gulab jamun—saffron-flavored doughy treats—though there was barely enough time to prepare the milk solids for the khoya base ingredient. It was a specialty she'd learned to bake for Diwali that could come in handy now.

Before lunch, Shreya called Aliania over to her house to try on the beginnings of her dress. When the kit returned home, she looked thrilled but refused to share anything.

"And Grammy is going to help me with something *extra*-special," Ali said, sauntering to her room. "For a surprise."

Taliya hesitated over the note she was sending to Samson about their flight arrival, nervous over what in the world Ali could be planning as a surprise. If her grandmother was involved, at least some adult would keep the kit in check. Thinking about all that made her add a note to Samson about the expansive size of the wedding now and how dressy it had become, since he was standing up with them to officiate.

> I am aware. I packaged the sari, though
> the president selected it personally. I will
> send you a photo this afternoon of the
> attire I have chosen.

Ali will appreciate that. She's gotten very dictatorial. I'm grateful for the beautiful sari. It was so sweet of the president to send it.

Of course she sent a gift. Padme is frustrated she cannot attend in person.

Taliya's hackles spiked all the way up the back of her head at the thought that the president of the United States even considered attending their potluck, hastily thrown-together wedding. *Oh gods.* They were friends—on a first-name basis in private—but she was still freaking President Padme Nakobi, incredibly powerful and important, especially to tigran.

A message came in from Marla.

Parth's parents heard about the ceremony and are wondering if they can come. They've never been to a wedding.

Neither have I! Taliya huffed.

Of course. They are more than welcome.

She couldn't remember exactly where Parth's parents lived, but it wasn't local. Though if Marla's parents had survived the Gathering, she would have invited them too, no matter where in the world they lived. The sneaking anxiety that someone was going to be overlooked tingled in Taliya's whiskers.

Amrita raced past her. "Grammy needs me!"

She was out the door before Taliya could even acknowledge that. Then her com buzzed with six messages, each from a guest excited for the event. She took a deep breath, whoofed it out, and set about responding.

After lunch, Shreya came to the main house and pulled Taliya aside. "Join me for a walk."

"Right now?"

Taliya's com buzzed seven times in a row. Probably more of the neighbors trying to coordinate the food offerings, despite her encouraging them to trust the "luck" process. Or at least leave her out of it. She glanced at the living room, where the kits were arguing over what to watch on the media wall. Shreya ended the debate by shutting the system down—to the offended squalls of the trio.

"If you're going to fight, no one watches anything for thirty minutes. To your rooms, shut the door, and read until then."

Little Jai opened his mouth like he was going to complain, but the girls had already started toward their bedrooms, knowing better than to argue with Grammy when she was annoyed. He dragged his feet down the hall and slammed his door.

"This is one reason why we limited you and your brothers," Shreya said, turning back to her daughter. "Avoids the bickering."

The sudden silence was a relief, but the kits rarely

argued that much about media. They were just all hopped-up on the stress simmering around the property.

"Can we be back from this walk in thirty minutes?" Taliya said. "You know Ali has set a timer."

"Yes. It's fine. We're not going far."

Taliya followed her mother out the door and sent the dogs inside with the command to guard the kits. She watched as the dark-furred Belgian Malinois trotted down the hall—noses in the air, searching for their subjects—and then sat outside the bedrooms. It wasn't really necessary, but if the walk ran long, Cairo and Elektra would be a good distraction.

At the bottom of the porch stairs, Shreya linked her arm through Taliya's and started toward the forest. Taliya's head spun with what in the world this could be about. She certainly didn't require the wedding-night "sex talk" from her mother. Maybe there was no way to accomplish creating all the outfits, or Aliania was being demanding. But they shouldn't need to head into the woods to discuss that. Did they have to be out of hearing range from both houses?

"Calm down," Shreya said, patting her daughter's arm. "There's just something we need to retrieve. Ali asked to see pictures from my wedding, and there's no getting around it now."

Taliya tried to remember ever seeing wedding photos of her parents, but nothing came to mind. It had been the spring almost two years before she was born, though they'd been together as mates for several years. Probably coming up on a twenty-fifth anniversary of some kind. Just before Kerkaw stirred up trouble for tigran. Her father was still a teacher, and her mother was the school administrator.

"Your father and I lived a *highly* civilized life back then," Shreya said. "Deeply entrenched in human society. We decided to get married when we were ready for kits because that was the accepted thing to do. But we already knew what we had was forever."

"Father must have loved planning it all." She could imagine him researching and studying various human traditions. "I have to admit, if you've told me about the wedding, I don't remember."

"It was a disaster."

"What?" Taliya stopped and pulled her mother to a halt. "Why?"

"We tried to make too many people happy. Mostly, that day is a blur to me, but everyone had an opinion on what we should or shouldn't have done."

Taliya could understand that feeling.

Shreya sighed and started walking again, leading Taliya farther into the trees. "Some humans we worked with were offended because we leaned on our Indian heritage for the clothing and food. And they weren't subtle or quiet about it. Maybe they were expecting more American traditions because of your father's studies. But we definitely didn't get it right. Politics were already starting to shift around tigran living free, so maybe that fed into it."

"How awful."

"Well, the day itself was awful in many ways, but we were married and excited to start a family so didn't worry too much once it was over. Our coworkers moved on to complaining about something else. But it's probably why I never talk much about the ceremony and fuss around it."

Shreya stopped at a walnut tree and began eyeing the ground at the base of the trunk. "It's here somewhere."

She squatted near a large rock, moved it aside, and pulled a spade out of her pocket to dig into the earth.

"You buried something out here?" Taliya kneeled next to her.

Shreya nodded. "When the first hints of the Gathering began, we started hiding anything of value. If we had to run, the Enforcers would never find it. There's a stash of antique coins out here we should probably recover too."

The spade clinked on something metal, and Shreya scraped around the sides of a two-foot by two-foot box. With a bit more digging, she dragged it from the hiding place, dusted the top, and opened the lid.

Taliya was more shocked than she'd been at the presidential sari. "Are those from your wedding?"

Shreya wiped her hand on her slacks and sat crisscross before lifting an intricately detailed, heavy-looking gold necklace into the light. The top portion was like elaborate lace made of metal, and from that hung dozens of thick strands with ruby gems at the ends.

"This set belonged to my grandmother. The story is that my grandfather traded work building a jewelry store for these fine pieces—the necklace, three bracelets, and a headpiece designed to wrap around tigran ears."

In general, tigran didn't wear jewelry at all. Taliya had never owned a single item. Her first thought was that Ali was going to lose her little mind over the beautiful jewelry. The second thought was how perfect the dozen small red stones throughout the set would look against the dark-green sari.

Shreya handed her the necklace with a soft smile. "Try it on."

Taliya had been right about the weight of the piece. It had to be manufactured gold, so not as valuable as the old-school products, but still a bulky five pounds. She wrapped it around her neck and hooked the back into place. It covered her throat completely, and the strands hung several inches down onto her shoulders and chest.

"Perfect fit," Shreya said before adding the thinner matching headdress and resting the bindi with a large red gem on her daughter's forehead.

Taliya touched the stone. "Does it look okay?"

Shreya smiled gently and sniffled, adjusting the necklace and then squeezing her daughter's shoulders. "It's lovely, kitten. Like they were made for you. But let's pack it back up so they can be a surprise for the family."

"This isn't the surprise Ali is excited about?" Taliya removed the necklace and reluctantly placed it back in the box.

Shreya chuckled. "No. But that will be delightful too." She replaced the headdress, closed the box, and stood up.

"I'll keep this in my room so no one stumbles across it. I can't wait to see Ali's face."

"She's going to be annoyed she doesn't have any beautiful jewelry to wear too," Taliya said, joining her mother in the walk back to the house.

"Well, she'll just have to look forward to when she's a bride herself. As much as she's the instigator, this wedding is *your* day to shine."

TUESDAY FLEW BY IN A WHIRLWIND OF TIDYING BOTH HOUSES TO get them "company ready," cleaning up the lawn and flowers around the property, and responding to messages of guests saying they were attending or suggestions surrounding the potluck. Taliya was beginning to understand why brides often freaked out over all the details, constant well-meant concerns, and opinions flying at them. With nearly all the invitations answered, there hadn't been a single decline. They were getting close to reenacting the jam-packed final movie scene that had inspired Aliania. It was good the event was being done quickly because dragging it out over weeks or months would have made all of Taliya's fur fall out with the stress.

Wednesday morning, the tables, chairs, cool blowers, and serving items were delivered, and the canopy was set up by four nervous-looking humans from the company who rushed off the minute they were done. Tuscan and Tyler took charge of setting up around the yard—tables along the outside edges and chairs in rows for the ceremony that could then be moved for the afterparty.

Taliya stood on the porch, a black cat she'd never noticed before weaving around her ankles and rubbing on her legs. She gave it a head scritch and then tried to imagine the lawn covered with guests. Thirty yards of grass lay between the main house and her parents' home, but the tree line formed a barrier at one end. At the other end, they would need to figure out parking for dozens of vehicles. Parth had volunteered to direct that during the arrivals.

Kano clomped up the steps, making the cat skitter away, and wrapped Taliya up in a hug. "Everything is fine. Everything will be fine."

"I just want Thursday at six o'clock to get here," she mumbled into his chest. "Then there's nothing more to plan, and it will just be what it is."

"True." He kissed the top of her head and leaned back to look at her. "And then we can get back to our normal lives until Ali thinks up another way to make us batty."

"Oh gods. This should fill her quota for the year."

"That's very optimistic of you."

Kano turned to stand next to her with an arm around her waist. "You know, the traditional bride and groom can withstand all this stress because they know their lives will be together afterward. That big leap into marriage awaits them."

"We kind of had that transition forced onto us at the facility."

"Kind of? Absolutely forced. But I've never been co-erced into a better happily ever after."

Taliya chuffed lovingly at him, wrapped her tail around his leg, and tucked closer under his arm. "That's what we should focus on. Making the public commitment to a marriage without any fear or desperation or threat. Even our handfasting was under duress, not something we planned."

"So let's celebrate this totally legal, totally chosen ceremony."

"And overlook the fact that our eldest basically manipulated us into it."

"Definitely," Kano said. "Let's just say she had a great idea, and we are excited to embrace it."

Tuscan started the planned playlist on the sound system, and all three kits came out of the house to see what was happening. Aliania immediately raced into the field to dance, followed by Amrita and Little Jai.

"Help your uncles with the chairs!" Kano called out to them. If they heard over the music, they ignored him.

Taliya's com buzzed, and she pulled it from her pocket. "Samson says the plane is ready to leave. They'll be at the airport here in a couple of hours."

"How's Reynaldo doing? He's still coming, right?"

"Says he wouldn't miss it."

"We'll have to trust Carl to handle it, if the crowd is too much."

The dogs joined in the dancing, leaping around and barking, and Taliya smiled up at her soon-to-be-legal husband. "C'mon." Dragging him by the hand, they joined the kits on the lawn, tails swishing and hips rocking with the deep rhythms and electronic melody of the pop music. Ali pretended to be embarrassed by her parents but allowed Kano to scoop her up like they were going to waltz and twirl her around, feet flying as she squealed. She was almost too big for such silliness, but not quite yet.

After three more songs, Taliya admitted defeat and staggered over to sit on the porch steps. Grampa Jai had come out of his house and was enjoying the impromptu dance party from a chair on his own porch. Shreya didn't join him, and Taliya worried her mother was exhausting herself with trying to make perfect outfits for everyone. It was tempting to demand she come outside and play a bit, but Taliya had been forbidden to enter her parents' home until after the wedding. Secret projects were hidden away there.

When a slow song began—which all the adults had insisted on adding to the playlist for snack breaks and rests—the dancers groaned and the dogs settled at Grampa Jai's feet. Amrita and Little Jai flopped down in the grass, panting, but Ali and Kano headed to the smokehouse near the tree line. He'd been preparing several substantial racks of pork ribs for a feast that night after Samson, Carl, and Reynaldo arrived. Wheeling out the black metal smoker, he and Aliania laid them out and added wood chips to start the final cooking. Tuscan and Tyler joined him, mostly trying to sneak bits of meat off the end of the slabs.

"That smells amazing. I'm starving!" Amrita called out without lifting her head.

"I could eat a horse!" Little Jai chimed in. "The whole thing."

Amrita laughed. "Yuck! Not the hooves."

"I'd gnaw on those hooves." He pretended to do just that with dramatic *rawr rawr* noises.

This gained him the desired gagging sounds from his sisters.

"Not horse. Pig!" Aliania yelled at him. "But you have to wait till dinner."

Amrita sat up. "And we are far too civilized to ever eat a *horse*. Right, Grampa?"

"Correct," Grampa Jai said from his porch chair. "I hear it's pretty tough meat, anyhow."

Little Jai energetically resumed his gnawing noises until Amrita ran away to hide behind her grampa.

Taliya's twin brothers began setting up a dome next to their house for sleeping that night while the expected trio from Washington took over their rooms, reminding her it wouldn't be long before they arrived.

"Leftovers from last night are coming out," Taliya said, getting up from the porch step. "If you're hungry for lunch, let's go."

Amrita and Little Jai hurriedly did just that. Taliya waited until they were inside to add, "And then showers and cleanup." This was greeted by the expected *awwws* of annoyance. "We have friends already on their way, and you two are stinky little kits."

"I'll shower while you eat." Aliania thundered past them and sing-songed, "Guests are coming!"

Taliya repressed a smirk at the idea of Ali wanting to look good for Samson. At least one of them wasn't going to fight her on becoming presentable for the "uncles." Gods help all of them tomorrow when it was time to dress for the wedding. Most brides didn't have three offspring to contend with. She hoped the excitement of fancy outfits Grammy had personally created would make preparations smoother.

CHAPTER 3

The rental transport from the airport pulled onto the property at two thirty pm. All three kits raced from the house screaming at the first bark from Cairo announcing the arrival. Taliya set down her com and followed them out, hoping the enthusiastic greeting wouldn't overwhelm Reynaldo. Kano was outside, fussing with the ribs in the smoker. He waved and closed the lid before heading over to join the welcome.

Samson pulled into his usual spot on the side of the house. Carl, in the front passenger seat, threw his door open before the engine was shut down. With a deep growl, he matched Amrita and Little Jai's excitement, grabbing each one and tossing them in the air while they shrieked. It was a routine game on his visits, but Taliya noticed Carl stretching his back afterward. The twins were getting awfully big for throwing around. Or Carl was getting too old. She refused to contemplate the second option.

"Whew," Carl said, tugging at his collar, "I always forget how hot and muggy it is here. How do you stand it?"

"You have to pant, Uncle Carl," Little Jai said, "like this." He demonstrated with his tongue hanging out, and Carl laughed.

Amrita shoved her twin. "Humans don't pant, you fur ball. And we have air conditioning."

Carl panted dramatically anyhow, just to hear them shriek again.

Aliania waited by Samson's door for him to exit the vehicle, her tail whipping back and forth. She was wearing her favorite top and slacks, a vibrant blue that matched her eyes. *Gods help me with this one.*

Samson unfolded his hulking eight-foot frame from the transport and gave her a chaste side-hug. Taliya choked up a little at how careful he was being to stay avuncular. Ali was only six, but as a tigran that meant five feet tall with a feminine figure beginning to form. It surely wasn't lost on Samson that his honorary niece had a crush on him and needed to be treated affectionately but guardedly.

Taliya made it to the vehicle as Reynaldo climbed out of the back seat. Their eyes met, and he slow-blinked at her before accepting a hug. She fought back sad tears at how thin the once-vibrant panthran was. And happy tears that he was alive and safe now, after so long. Under the scents of travel and anxiety, he still smelled like her friend Rey, the master dragon wrangler. When she realized the hug had possibly gone on too long, Taliya reluctantly released him with a chuff.

"It's so good to see you in person again," she said, squeezing his arms like that could somehow restore his muscles and strength.

Rey smiled. "It's wonderful to be here. I could use a good party."

"Oh, yeah," Kano said, "there's gonna be a par-tay." The two males paused awkwardly for a moment—reminding Taliya they barely knew each other—before turning to Carl at the front of the vehicle with a kit under each arm.

"Rey," Carl said, "you probably remember Amrita and Jai. They were awfully tiny last time you saw them in person. Kits, this is my mate Reynaldo."

They'd heard many stories about him over the years and seen him on video calls recently, but the pair stared at Rey in person with wide eyes. Samson was the only creature they knew who wasn't a tigran. This massive black panthran male with deep-golden eyes—even in his emaciated state—had them gawking.

Amrita studied Carl's face, then glanced back at Rey and grinned. "You match."

"I supposed we do," Carl said with a chuckle.

Reynaldo smiled down at them. "It is very nice to see you both again."

Carl gave a surprised grunt as Tuscan and Tyler

jumped him from behind, nearly tackling him to the ground and knocking Amrita and Jai to the side amid squeals and growls.

"Boys!" Shreya hollered from her front door. "Don't break him!"

The twins obediently let go and acted like he'd managed to shake them off, falling into the grass dramatically. Yet another game and tradition that needed rethinking. When they were smaller, Carl could wrestle with them both. Now, they were as tall as him, though still gangly. But still tigran.

Carl laughed. "One at a time, at least." He bent over and put his hands on his knees. "This old soldier is going to need to up his workouts before my next visit."

Shreya started across the lawn toward them, with Grampa Jai following. "Let's get your bags inside and you settled," she said, "before you melt in this heat or my offspring maim you."

Moving to the back of the transport—and leaving a disappointed-looking Aliania behind—Samson pulled hanging bags that must contain their wedding attire from the trunk. For that day of travel, Reynaldo and Samson were wearing lightweight tunics and slacks, while Carl was in his casual camo. Kano grabbed the two small suitcases, and Carl hauled a canvas shopping bag from the back seat. He'd messaged about wanting to add to the potluck offerings, and Taliya wondered what he had planned. It was a secret, according to Carl, or the luck of it would be tarnished. He probably knew more about the tradition than any of them.

The T-twins stood up and stared at Reynaldo. "I remember you from school at the camp," Tuscan said.

"You do?" Rey looked pleased. "That feels like a dozen lifetimes ago."

"Before you started working with the dragons," Tyler added.

Rey nodded. "Among other things."

Taliya wanted to shift that conversation immediately, so she headed the group across the lawn, like Shreya had requested.

Leaning close to her, Rey whispered, "How do you tell them apart? I never could."

"They're identical," Taliya admitted, which wasn't a thing for tigers and came from the human DNA. "But over time, just their mannerisms give them away."

"I hope I have the time to discover that."

She linked an arm through his. "Me too. Come meet my parents."

The rest of the afternoon was spent visiting and talking about the wedding. Shreya had somehow managed to make iced tea and chicken salad sandwiches for their guests to refresh after their trip. Carl and Kano enjoyed male bonding over the ribs on the smoker while the group gathered on the main house porch, aiming the cool blowers that direction. Essentially outdoor air conditioning was a treat Taliya considered buying as a permanent summer installment. Aliania regaled them all with how her simple plan had become a community celebration.

"Honestly," Taliya admitted, "we haven't decided much about the actual ceremony. All the planning has gone into the party side of things."

Samson nodded thoughtfully. "Then we will need to rehearse and all be on the same page."

"That's what today is traditionally for," Grampa Jai said as Amrita climbed into his lap to escape her feisty twin brother. "You have a rehearsal of the proceedings, and then the family and wedding party join together for a special meal."

Samson took charge and insisted, in lawyerly fashion, that they should discuss and practice exactly how the ceremony itself would unfold. "With the whole community attending, we should get organized."

Taliya suspected he wanted to make sure they provided a good example for how creature weddings could be accomplished.

Chairs were already set up on the lawn facing the tree line, and an arch covered in colorful flowers would be delivered tomorrow for them to stand under during the actual wedding. Aliania explained that much as Samson nodded with understanding. He had Taliya and Kano stand in place, and her fur spiked with unexpected excitement. Kano made a low rumble.

"Tuscan and Tyler," Samson said, "you are standing up with your sister and Kano like you did at the handfasting, right?"

They nodded and joined the pair at the altar.

"You know," Tuscan said, standing behind Kano, "when we first met you, we both wanted to bite you."

Tyler nodded intently. "Hard. Lots of blood."

Tuscan made a growling chomp and clicked his teeth.

Kano whuffed. "Why?"

"Well," Tuscan said, "we had thoughts and feelings about some strange male who'd been messing with our sister."

Taliya snorted a laugh, remembering when they'd been reunited during the escape from the breeding facility and watching her brothers' little faces as they made the connection between her round stomach and Kano living with her in the cell. She fully believed they'd been ready to defend her, even if they were only six and barely came up to Kano's chest.

"But we didn't," Tyler said, moving to stand behind Taliya, "because you were kinda enormous and scary. And you made us feel safe during the trip to the camp. So we agreed not to bite you right away."

Tuscan gave Kano a gentle shoulder punch. "Yeah. You turned out to be worthy."

"I'm grateful," Kano said, looking very serious, "because you had sharp little teeth."

The twins grinned with a glint in their eyes, fangs flashing white.

"There will be no biting at this wedding," Shreya said, pointing at each of her sons. "Behave yourselves."

"Agreed," Samson said, giving each twin a stern look.

"That settled, is anyone else standing up with the couple?"

"Me! Wait for me."

Marla rushed up the aisle between the arranged chairs. Taliya grimaced at what pain from poorly healed POW abuse and declawing must be leading to the mincing steps of her best friend, but Marla was all smiles. The human-looking tigran stopped in front of the group expectantly.

"Aliania messaged to say I needed to get here immediately. I see why now. Hello, Samson."

"Good to see you, Marla. Traditionally, the female friends stand next to the bride."

As Marla stepped into place beside her, urging Tyler to take a few steps back, Taliya's heart raced. Things would look unbalanced if Kano didn't have a male friend standing with him too. If Parth had arrived with Marla, he wasn't in sight. And the two males weren't exactly chummy. Sudden sadness that Kano didn't have a buddy to stand up with him made tears threaten.

"General Thompson," Kano said.

They made eye contact, and Kano gave a backward tilt of his head, asking Carl to stand with him without a word spoken. Carl gave a nod in return and moved into place amid some friendly jostling with Tuscan. Reynaldo sat in the front row with Grampa Jai and Shreya, who had Amrita and Little Jai on chairs between them. Aliania stood in the second row, an expectant look on her face that made Taliya's heart rate pick up again.

"Don't fuss, Mama," Ali said. "I know exactly what I'll be doing during the ceremony."

"That doesn't make me feel more at ease." Taliya looked at Kano, and he smiled with a small shake of his head.

Shreya cleared her throat. "Samson, none of us has ever been to India or an Indian wedding. Or an American one, for that matter. What Jai and I included in our ceremony was from interweb research and parts we thought were interesting."

"Weddings are what we decide to make them," Samson said, looking at the bride, then the groom. "How *you* want to celebrate this legal union is all that matters."

"I think we can skip a lot of the religious portions." Taliya frowned. "No red dust in my fur. And I have no idea how henna anywhere on my body could possibly work."

Kano nodded. "Agreed."

"But you *must* have the flower necklaces," Aliania said.

"The thick ones we saw in the videos?" Taliya asked.

Aliania smiled. "I already ordered them with the other flowers. Like I said, don't worry. It's covered. Samson knows when that will happen in the service."

Taliya and Kano looked at him, and Samson tipped his head in acknowledgement.

"Okay, then." Taliya inhaled, whuffed out a breath, and looked back at her daughter. "Did you write the vows?"

Ali pursed her whiskers. "No. Of course not."

"You do not actually need them," Samson said. "The

legal requirements are very brief. Agreement is all that matters. The rest is up to you."

Taliya glanced up at Kano, and he chuffed. "I have a few things I'd like to say to you."

He took her hands, the warmth from his touch easing up her arms and making her skin tingle.

"I suppose I have a few things I could say to you as well."

Samson pulled out his com and checked it. "From what Aliania sent me, you are planning a mostly standard American ceremony with some Indian elements added in."

Her parents looked back at her, and Ali grinned. "You weren't even talking about it," she said in her own defense. "I took care of it."

Taliya shrugged. "Why not. However, I would like veto power."

"Fine." Ali folded her arms across her chest. "But for everything you veto, I get another portion of ribs at dinner."

Tuscan laughed. "Not from my share you don't!"

Samson returned his com to his pocket and cleared his throat loudly. "If anyone is going to enjoy dinner, we need to finish this rehearsal."

The scent of the meal in the smoker across the yard wafted past them, and the group focused back on Samson with smiles and obedient attention.

TALIYA AWOKE THAT SUNNY THURSDAY MORNING TO AN EMPTY house. In the kitchen, breakfast was done and cleaned up. It felt rather like someone had been plotting behind her back to provide a quiet morning for the bride. She made some chai and headed to the porch. The cool blowers were in place around the yard, making the summer morning heat and humidity a bit more tolerable.

Outside, the whole family and their overnight guests were waiting with a HAPPY BIRTHDAY! banner hung across the chairs on the lawn. A few wrapped gifts sat on a porch table.

"Mama!" Amrita and Little Jai spotted her first.

"Happy Birthday!" the rest of the group shouted as the dogs leapt up and barked in surprise at the loud noise.

Kano rose from the Adirondack chair and gave his stunned mate a hug. "Did you think we'd forget?"

She laughed. "Well, I certainly did!"

"I know we don't often have a party," Shreya said, "but this birthday feels extra-special."

Carl lifted his glass that smelled like it contained strong coffee. "Happy twenty-first, Taliya!"

"Come and sit," Kano said, leading her to the chair he'd vacated. "We have presents for you."

Taliya couldn't imagine when any of this planning had taken place, and Kano seemed terribly pleased with the surprise. Amrita and Jai had gotten her a set of deep-purple tunic and slacks. Her parents and brothers gave her a dozen new chickens for the coop, and Aliania had selected three pairs of fuzzy socks with paw prints on the bottom. Samson had commissioned a watercolor painting of their homestead, which everyone agreed was perfect. Carl and Reynaldo proudly displayed the three large bee-hive brood boxes they'd had delivered—and her parents had hidden—so Taliya could start the colony she'd been planning.

"This is all so wonderful." Taliya sighed deeply and smiled at her friends and family. "A perfect start to the day."

"There's one more present," Ali said.

Kano handed Taliya a jewelry box that fit in the palm of her hand. Based on the fact Aliania was all but wiggling out of her seat, Taliya anticipated something special.

"We hadn't talked about this part," he said, "but the family agreed you deserve the traditional bride gift."

Taliya opened the lid on the dark-blue box to reveal an oval, two-inch black onyx stone surrounded by a border of filigree gold. She lifted it from the box by the long gold chain, and everyone *oooed* and smiled.

"Don't put it on yet," Kano said. "It's your bride neck-lace. I'll officially place it around your neck during the ceremony, but I wanted you to see it now. Make sure you approve."

Taliya admired the polished stone glinting in the sunlight. "It's amazing. I hope I'm allowed to wear it more than just today."

"Never take it off!" Aliania squealed, hands clenched under her chin.

"That may be excessive," Shreya said, "but definitely don't wait for special occasions to wear it."

Reynaldo nodded and quietly added, "Celebrate every day. Enjoy the beautiful things. We all know it can change in a moment."

That sobering thought brought silence to the group, and Rey shifted with a huff. "Sorry. I didn't mean to upset you."

Taliya chuffed at him. "No. You just reminded us. I celebrated my eighteenth birthday in a refugee camp. We should be grateful for every moment of freedom and never take it for granted."

"To freedom." Carl raised his glass again, and the others joined his toast with whatever drink they had in hand.

Samson rumbled deep in his chest. "Today, we exercise that freedom by celebrating and seeing Taliya and Kano legally married. With all the rights we creatures deserve."

That gained another toast and drink from the group.

"And Happy Birthday, Taliya." Samson said. "Here is to many, many more."

CHAPTER 4

Taliya took a moment to evaluate her image in the bedroom mirror. Her mother had spent the afternoon at the main house, keeping the kits busy and helping them get ready so Taliya could have time to herself. A long, uninterrupted shower. A hot cup of chai as she brushed her fur until it shone. Finally, putting on the wedding sari Padme had sent, pinning and tucking every piece into place.

The forest-green fabric looked fantastic against her orange fur, and the gold trim with black embroidery running through it picked up her stripes. Sparkles and spangles in the trim caught the light as she turned to examine it from every angle. Pulling the silky, sheer black dupatta with green and gold trim over her head, she chuckled at how her ears were two bumps under the fabric. But the colors around her face made her golden eyes shimmer.

She had to admit, she looked every inch the bride.

Outside, the rumble of conversations and random clunks of tables or chairs being moved let her know final preparations were underway. The only food smells she noticed were rehearsal dinner leftovers from lunch and something oniony and cheesy with potatoes mixed in—possibly what Carl was preparing. It didn't seem like the guest arrivals and potluck offerings had begun.

Inside, kits pattered up and down the hallway with giggling and teasing. They'd decided Taliya had to wait until the ceremony started to see their outfits, and she was fine with letting Shreya handle that side of the event. Aliania surely wouldn't allow anything she didn't approve of to take place.

It felt like just yesterday but also another lifetime ago that she and Kano had stood before Samson in the campfire area of the refugee camp and agreed to be handfast. That ceremony had been out of desperate necessity to keep their combined family together in the foreign place. Kano and Aliania joining Taliya and her brothers, along with the unborn twins she was carrying. None of them could have anticipated how their lives would stay intertwined and lead to this moment. She'd only been seventeen then. Clueless about being a wife and mother. It was all a bit surreal.

Taliya could imagine another life. One where the Gathering never happened. Where she and Anya—the best friend who'd vanished, along with other tigran—graduated from school together and went on double dates. A life where Kano's wife wasn't murdered. Where Taliya never met him at all. Would she have been happier in that alternate reality? One where she had offspring by choice and was sheltered from the worst of human greed?

There would be no Amrita or Little Jai or Aliania. No Marla. I'd never have flown on a dragon. Never been an ambassador for tigran around the world. Never met Carl or Rey or Samson. And what mate could be more amazing than Kano?

When life gives you shit, make fertilizer. Taliya wasn't sure where she'd heard that before, but it had certainly proven true in her own experience. Out of the horror of oppression, sadness, and genocide had come family, friends, and love—nourishment to enrich the joy of her home.

A knock on the door brought her back to the moment. Glancing at her remarkably quiet com, she realized it was five thirty. *Almost time.*

"Come in."

Shreya peeked through a crack in the bedroom door, caught sight of her daughter, and whuffed back tears. "Oh, kitten. You look wonderful." She slipped in, holding the box they'd dug up in the woods, and closed the door firmly behind her, making sure no one followed. "I ventured over to the frat house and got the jewelry."

Kano had spent the afternoon across the lawn at her parents' home, with Samson, Carl, Reynaldo, Tuscan, Tyler, and Grampa Jai. The image of them all drinking ale and being extra-male like fraternity brothers made Taliya smile. She hoped none of them were too drunk, though that could make things interesting.

Shreya set the box on the bed and opened it. They both admired the wedding set for a moment before Shreya lifted the necklace out and placed it around Taliya's neck, fastening it and readjusting the dupatta again. The weight of it reminded Taliya that they were accomplishing something important today. Turning to look in the mirror, she couldn't help but grin, fangs and all. The outfit was just ridiculously and delightfully ostentatious.

"Now the headpiece," Shreya said, lifting it from the box.

Taliya lowered the dupatta so her mother could arrange the gold strands around her ears and rest the ruby stone on her forehead. They both looked at her reflection in the mirror again.

Shreya sighed. "I wish the stone was black, like the necklace Kano's giving you."

"No, it's perfect." Taliya pulled the dupatta back into place before adding the three thick matching bracelets to her left wrist. "Even having wedding jewelry is beyond what I'd expected."

"Glad we could up our game to match that sari," Shreya said and pursed her whiskers. "I know this whole wedding has become far more than you imagined when you agreed to it, but I doubt you'll have any regrets."

Taliya looked at her mother through the mirror image and frowned. "I'd never regret marrying Kano."

"No, no, I mean the ceremony and party. When it's all

done, it will be worth the fuss and bother. So many wonderful memories."

Voices came from outside, along with the aroma of spicy food. They both glanced at the window, but the curtains were drawn.

"And it sounds like your guests are arriving," Shreya said, giving her daughter's hand a squeeze.

After a quick knock on the door, Marla peeked in and squealed at the sight of her friend. "Oh, great gods!" She giggled, slipped into the room, and leaned against the door to shut it. "You look like something out of a magazine."

"You look amazing yourself," Taliya said.

As planned, Marla was wearing a black two-piece outfit from Taliya's fancy government work wardrobe. Shreya had adjusted it a bit because Marla was only five foot ten, though she was stocky for a human female—the tigran DNA peeking out. The gauzy fabric shimmered and glistened in the light as she spun slowly to show off. Marla had even put on a bit of makeup with red lipstick, which she never wore, and styled her long, dark hair in an elaborate updo. She noticed Taliya gawking at it and touched the side of her head.

"Too much?"

"Absolutely not. I'm just wondering how you accomplished it."

"Like *I* could do this." Marla huffed a laugh. "A hairdresser in town is to thank, but I don't imagine it will survive much past the ceremony and photos. I plan to dance and party. Bobby pins will be flying everywhere."

"Aunty Marla!" Aliania called from the hallway. "You are supposed to *wait*!"

"Sorry," Marla called back. "I just couldn't!"

"Grammy," Ali shouted, "you need to get dressed. Get out here! Both of you."

Shreya flicked her tail. "You have a very dictatorial wedding planner."

"I most certainly do," Taliya agreed. "Tiny, but mighty." *Though not even that tiny anymore.*

"Well, I suppose we must obey . . . or suffer the consequences." Shreya gently hugged her daughter, then straightened the sari. "You have fifteen minutes until showtime." She adjusted the gem on Taliya's forehead, gave her a kiss on the cheek, and slipped out the door before Aliania could yell again.

Marla started to follow, but hesitated and turned back to Taliya. "I can't be grateful for the Gathering and the pain that came from that. However, I'm eternally grateful it brought us together. I wish I could have hidden you better. But it all leads to us here, now."

"I've been thinking about the same things. So much sadness, leading to so much happiness." Taliya swallowed hard. "I wish I could have hidden you too and protected you."

Marla smiled sadly, looking for a moment like she was miles away. She sniffled and blotted a tear from her cheek. "You're gonna make me ruin this expensive makeup."

"Well," Taliya walked over and wrapped her arms around her best friend. "We can't have that. Unless it's happy tears."

Marla returned the hug. "Only *happy* ones." She opened the door to leave, and Taliya caught a glimpse of Aliania in the hallway, ready to bang on the door. "I'm coming, you bossy thing, you."

Ali gasped and slapped a hand across her eyes dramatically. "I don't want to see her yet!"

Marla chuckled and closed the door behind her. A warm sense of peace washed over Taliya as Aunty Marla and Aliania bickered in the hallway before heading to the front door. She turned back toward the mirror for one final inspection. There was nothing to do but wait for Aliania to tell her it was time. She checked her com, and there were already several notifications of photos from what was beginning out on the lawn. It was tempting to scroll through, but Ali wanted the flowers and final setup to be a surprise. Based on the cacophony of conversation and food scents from outside now, she could tell the neighbors were arriving.

The music on the sound system changed to tunes that were part of the ceremony introduction and a signal for Tuscan and Tyler to make sure everyone took their seats. Butterflies launched in Taliya's stomach and fluttered up into her throat. It was silly to be nervous. She'd given public talks in front of foreign dignitaries and crowds of thousands. Sometimes hostile crowds. Taking a deep breath, she calmed and centered herself. Everyone out there was a friend, and they'd come to celebrate with her family. All Taliya had to do was remember what she'd decided on for her vows. Pondering that set the butterflies in motion again.

After three solid raps on the door, Ali said, "Mama, it's time."

Taliya thought she had five more minutes, but of course Aliania would want her in place before the last second. She opened the door and faced her eldest.

Ali covered her mouth with a gasp. "Oh, Mama. You look beautiful."

"Goodness. So do you."

Taliya took her daughter by the hands and stretched out her arms so she could appreciate the dress Shreya had created. It was a sleeveless sheath of silky forest-green that fell all the way to the floor. Around Ali's neck and on each wrist like a bracelet was a thick band of black fabric covered in green spangles that contrasted magnificently against her white fur. The kit stuck out a foot to reveal black slipper-style shoes like the ones Taliya had selected for herself.

"We have to keep them on until after dinner," Ali said. "I promise."

Unless required for safety or hiking, all of them went barefoot. It was much more comfortable for creature feet, but they were prepared to be civilized for the ceremony.

Motion from the front door caught her eye, and Taliya turned to find an unknown tigran, with what looked like a turn-of-the-last-century camera, snapping pictures of them.

"That's Joe," Ali said. "He wants to be a photographer and agreed to document things for us."

Taliya nodded at him, not sure which part was more confusing—the tigran photographer or a tigran named Joe. He raised the camera to his eye and snapped a couple more shots as they walked to the door. Marla was hovering near the living room window, watching the activity outside. Grampa Jai met them in the kitchen wearing his best navy-blue Diwali outfit with elaborate gold embroidery but no sparkly details. At the sight of his daughter in her bridal sari, he sighed loudly and placed a hand over his heart.

"Thanks," Taliya said, nervously adjusting the dupatta.

Clicking noises from Joe the photographer reminded her he was there, tucked off to the side but still recording the evening's events. She decided to ignore him unless otherwise instructed.

Giggling came from the back bedrooms, and Amrita and Little Jai thundered down the hall with Shreya calling for them to be careful and not fall down. The twins stopped short when they saw their mother in the kitchen.

"You're a princess!" Amrita said.

"As are you." Taliya fussed over Amrita's dress, which was just like Aliania's, and made a point of appreciating Little Jai's two-piece tunic and slacks that matched his grandfather's. He stood tall for a second, then ran to hide behind his grampa, all the attention too much.

Taliya's focus fell on Shreya, now dressed and ready as mother of the bride. "Mama, you can't possibly have made that this week."

Shreya dipped her head and smoothed her golden sari. "No. But I did make it. This is what I created for my own wedding. At first it felt funny to wear it for yours, but why not? The most beautiful outfit I've ever owned, and it just sits in a box."

"I insisted," Aliania said. "Once I saw it, boom."

Taliya nodded and smiled. "I agree."

Gauzy golden fabric wrapped around Shreya from top to bottom, even a pale-gold sheer dupatta. A simple gold chain with a ruby stone finished the ensemble, and Taliya realized it must be Shreya's bridal necklace, like what Kano would place around her own neck during the ceremony. Her mother adjusted it and smiled shyly. "I dug up a few more things."

"You look like an angel," Grampa Jai said, "just like the day I married you."

Taliya was amused and then a bit eeked out by the aroma of testosterone coming from her father. Aliania glanced back and forth between her grandparents and wrinkled her nose. "Ew! Stop that."

If the pair could blush, Taliya suspected they would.

"Well, then," Grampa Jai said, clapping his hands together, "are we all ready?"

Aliania peek out the front door and confirmed she was

satisfied with the outside group being in their assigned places. She motioned for the music to change, and what was playing faded out into some gentle European Renaissance-period music.

Shreya stepped onto the porch with the twins in front of her. The burst of awws from the guests reminded Taliya just how many tigran and others were out there. The butterfly swarm returned full force. She watched out the door as Reynaldo—wearing a navy suit with a dark-green tie—helped the three of them down the stairs to escort Shreya and the kits to their seats in the front row. They were quickly out of sight under the canopy.

Carl, in full formal military blues, rows of medals glinting in the sunlight, moved to the bottom of the porch stairs, and Marla turned to Taliya with a girlish glint in her eyes.

"See you out there," she whispered before standing tall and strutting out the door.

General Thompson helped her down the steps and led her toward the front, where Taliya knew Kano was waiting.

Grampa Jai cleared his throat dramatically. "Our turn." He held out his crooked elbow.

CHAPTER 5

Taliya could barely breathe—like she was wearing a corset, which seemed utterly ridiculous. She slipped her hand through her father's, struggling to keep her claws from poking out. They'd decided against a bouquet for her to carry, but now she wished for something to do with her hands. Gripping her father's arm with both of them, she forced a deep breath.

"Nervous?" Grampa Jai asked with a sly grin.

She whuffed. "Not about getting married. This is just … a lot."

"I know. But it will be over in fifteen minutes, and we can eat and party and celebrate with our whole community."

Without waiting for a response, he started out the door. The moment they stepped into view on the porch, all of the guests rose as one and turned to face them. A tangible wave of excitement hit her, and Taliya couldn't help but grin. Row after row of tigran faces smiled back. Their whole creature community was there and dressed in their most colorful attire—vibrant greens and blues, reds and oranges. When she managed to look past the bright rainbow of the guests, her knees nearly buckled.

Aliania had created a glorious altar scene, with orange and yellow marigolds, white roses, and dark greenery roped around the arch where Samson stood proudly in a dark suit and tie. Her brothers were wearing outfits that matched their father's, and Marla and Carl were in place. But she forgot all of it when Kano met her gaze.

The dark suit made every line on his face and the blue of his eyes stand out, even yards away. He was certainly the best-looking tigran to ever exist. As Marla once said, Taliya had won the husband lottery. He slow-blinked at her across the expanse of guests, and she returned it with a giggle. Suddenly, getting to him was all that mattered.

Grampa Jai gave her hands a squeeze, and they headed carefully down the steps. Parth was waiting to one side, in case Taliya needed extra help in the long sari, but she managed not to fall, despite shaky legs.

Before they turned to head down the aisle, Taliya spotted three drones hovering around the yard. Her father noticed her concern and whispered, "Say hello to the president."

Taliya gave the closest drone a small wave, and it bobbed up and down in response. When Taliya called Padme to thank her for the extraordinary gift, she'd extended an invitation to attend the wedding, never expecting it was logistically possible. Realizing the president had found a way to be there in spirit made Taliya stand up a little taller, ensuring the wedding ensemble was shown off to its best advantage.

Her father led her up the aisle between the seats, and she smiled at all the neighbors on either side as they passed by. The outfits weren't just colorful. She suspected everyone was wearing the fanciest ensembles they owned. Items pulled out for special celebrations. So much sparkle and elaborate decoration. When they reached the end, Grampa Jai squeezed her hands again and let go, moving to stand with her mother and the twins in the front row.

Taliya stepped into place and faced Kano. "Hi."

"Hi, yourself," he whispered back, eyes twinkling. "You look magnificent, wife."

"Thank you. Not so bad yourself, husband."

Samson cleared his throat with a chuckle, pulling their attention to him. "We have not confirmed those titles yet," he said with a wink.

The music faded out, and the crowd took their seats.

"Friends," Samson said in his deep, resonant voice. "Welcome to the first *legal wedding* of two creatures in nearly twenty years."

A cheer and several hoots went up from the crowd, and the wedding party laughed in response. Remembering the importance of what they were doing and why—beyond Ali's determination—helped still Taliya's nerves. Once again, she was in a position to be an example and ambassador for the species. Sharing that moment with their whole community was perfect.

Samson continued, "I am authorized to perform this ceremony . . . and any others that might be desired while I am in town." He glanced around the crowd and gave a serious tip of his head. "But today, we celebrate the legal union of my dear friends Taliya and Kano."

A happy squeal came from Aliania on the sidelines, waiting for her turn in the proceedings.

"The official, legal requirement is consent of both parties to this marriage." Samson turned to Taliya. "Do you take Kano as your husband?"

"I do," she said, like they'd seen in dozens of videos.

Samson turned to Kano. "And do you take Taliya as your wife?"

"I do," he said, "same as I did three years ago."

Samson gave a half smile. "When Taliya and Kano were handfast, I did all of the talking. Today, I will leave that to them. Kano, you may go first."

They hadn't shared their planned vows. Nervous energy tingled over Taliya's skin at what he might say.

Kano took her hands and stared at them as he spoke. "The moment those guards carried you into my cell in that dank, depressing underground prison, I knew every-thing was going to change. Listening to your uneven breathing as you unconsciously fought the sedation, I considered what our future would be. I couldn't imagine anything beyond the despair and sadness of what the scientists had planned. But then you woke up and were full of such fury and life. Such hope. I'd lost that. I'd lost so much." He glanced at Aliania with a small smile, then met Taliya's eyes.

"But you held that spark of survival we both needed. It lit a fire in me too. I can't put my finger on the moment I fell in love with you, but I remember when I knew I couldn't live without you. That moment we learned rescue was coming and I realized you could leave me. Could walk away and I'd never see you again." He rumbled across the space between them in that way she could feel but not hear.

"I'm so grateful I had the nerve to ask you not to. That we stayed together, despite the odds against us, and created a family. You are already my forever life-partner, my wife. But if we can symbolize one step in proving that creatures deserve civilized, legal marriages, then we will honor that as well. In front of our offspring, our families, and our community. We can't predict what the future holds, but I know we'll face it together. You and I and Aliania and Amrita and Little Jai. Our family."

Taliya chuffed gently at him, and he returned it with a slow-blink. Her chest ached, blazing with love for her amazing husband. In the front row, Shreya sniffled, and Amrita giggled.

Samson gave Kano a slight nod and smile, then shifted his attention to Taliya.

Following all of that eloquence felt impossible. Vows were planned, but she'd need to respond to what he'd said as well. Forget about the crowd watching and speak to her mate. She took a deep breath and squeezed Kano's hands, fighting to keep her claws from spiking out with nerves, though her tail thrashed. Tyler chuckled behind her, and Marla shushed him.

"Kano, if I brought you hope when we met, I can only say that you gave me courage. You reminded me that my goal was to survive. Whatever that required. And we did, despite all the odds against us so many times. You are absolutely right that everything changed when we met. I was a teenager, while you were mourning the loss of a wife. We were forced into each other's lives, and then became the core of each other's lives."

Kano flared his whiskers and smiled. From the front row, Shreya whuffed with a sob, and Taliya warmed with pride. That was the one line she was determined to work into her vows.

"There have been times I feared it would all fall apart. When I started training the dragons, and you were frustrated by how much of my time and attention that required. All of the separations we face because you need to travel for work, and I often do too. It hasn't been easy. It definitely hasn't been simple. But I can't imagine facing the future with anyone else. You are my partner, my mate, my husband. Forever."

From the look in Kano's eyes and the aromas wafting from him, she'd nailed it.

Taliya looked back to Samson, and he gave her a nod as well. Then he motioned for Aliania to come forward with the orange marigold garlands. She stood in front of her parents with one thick loop of flowers hanging from each arm.

"Calling on some Indian tradition," Samson said, "place the varmala around your mate's neck to symbolize your acceptance of this union."

Taliya took one first, trying not to laugh at the enthusiasm radiating off Aliania, her blue eyes fighting not to cross. Kano lowered his head, and she placed it around his neck. He took the other garland, giving Ali's hand a pat as he pulled away, and carefully placed it around Taliya's neck, tucking it under the dupatta. Their eyes met, and he sniffled back tears. That made some sneak into her own eyes, and she blinked rapidly to clear them.

Next, Aliania handed her father the jewelry box from that morning, and Kano opened it to remove Taliya's bridal necklace. He fastened it around her neck and adjusted the onyx stone to hang perfectly just below her collarbone. Ali giggled and hurried back down the aisle.

"By the power vested in me by the government of the United States," Samson said, "I now officially pronounce you husband and wife."

A cheer went up from the crowd of guests, and Taliya gave up trying to fight her tears, letting them roll down her face.

"Kiss!" Aliania screamed. "You have to kiss!"

Before Taliya could respond, Kano cupped her face with both hands and gave her a kiss that pulled her off balance and made the crowd cheer even louder. Then he pressed his forehead against hers to mingle their scents.

"I love you, wife."

"I love you too, husband."

She adored that those pet names were now legally true.

Celebratory music blasted from the sound system, deep rhythms vibrating through Taliya's chest and the ground around them. Kano crooked his arm, and she slipped hers through it as they headed back down the aisle, guests on both sides of them clapping with the music. But the pair stopped short at what awaited.

Standing at the end of the aisle with Reynaldo were Cairo and Elektra. Both dogs were decked out in a dark-green headdress, with orange marigolds hanging around their faces. As Rey released them and the dogs trotted toward the couple, Taliya realized they'd been painted too, . . . like elephants at a wedding. The well-trained Belgian Malinois' eyes were wide at the crowd and the noise, but they stopped obediently in front of their masters.

Kano chuckled, leaned down, and scratched the side of Cairo's face. "My poor man. What did they do to you?"

Cairo gave a yip, and his tongue lolled out. Elektra whined and sniffed at Taliya's sari.

"Let's go," Taliya said, motioning toward the house.

They started along the aisle again, elephant-dogs at their heels, but Aliania had another surprise in store. The crowd showered the happy couple with yellow and orange marigold petals. Taliya and Kano laughed as the colors and peppery fragrance rained down from all sides while the dogs chomped at the floaty bits.

Once they reached the porch steps, Taliya slipped under Kano's arm and hugged him, wrapping her tail around his legs. He curled his tail around her waist, slipped the dupatta onto her shoulders, and kissed the top of her head.

Mission accomplished!

While the music continued, each guest picked up their chair and moved it to the edge of the canopy to create an open section in the middle. Aliania had clearly coordinated the whole thing, though she still hovered and hurried a few creatures along with the transition. Joe, the tigran photographer, clicked away from his vantage point off to the side, and the presidential drones dove and swooped, catching every angle of the festivities. Taliya hoped the footage was being recorded. Ali commanded the dogs to lie down on the porch, and they obeyed.

"I think Ali may have a future as a wedding planner," Kano said, watching the next steps of the event unfold, and Taliya chuckled.

A family of tigran approached hesitantly, and Taliya remembered there was more formality expected. Guests needed to be greeted before they were directed to the potluck table—something she was excited to explore. She slipped from Kano's embrace as the music changed to a more soothing selection, and Taliya prepared to smile and shake hands, something she had years of experience with.

A loose line formed as each family shared their congratulations and then headed toward the long tables of food.

A handful of local humans had been invited, but glancing around, she realized none of them had attended. Carl was the only one in sight. And Marla, if you didn't know she only looked human. Maybe they'd felt as uncomfortable about being the minority in a crowd of creatures as she often felt in a crowd of humans.

Shreya and Grampa Jai flanked the newlyweds to chat happily with families they'd known for years, tigran she'd never met or didn't remember. Since the Gathering, families tended to stick close to their homesteads. Parth's parents seemed a bit overwhelmed by the large group, but it had been their idea to come.

Off to the side, Taliya noticed a couple of paunchy old male tigran, looking annoyed to be there. Neither approached to offer good wishes, though each had already managed to procure a large glass of her father's ale. Amrita and Little Jai raced past them, screaming for no apparent reason, and the males made sour faces before commenting to each other. Probably about the lack of respect and self-control in today's young ones. It made her chuckle, but she hoped they headed home soon, before the dancing started. She understood the need to invite the whole Ozark tigran community, but she didn't relish being judged by grumpy elders.

Finally, the congratulatory line was done, and the bride and groom were free to enjoy the wide variety of potluck offerings. A few tables had been set up, but most of the guests stood with their plates and chatted while they ate. Amrita sat on Uncle Carl's lap and shared a plate with Uncle Rey-Rey, as she'd already dubbed him. Little Jai sat next to them with Samson, munching away. Aliania was nowhere to be seen, but she could certainly handle getting her own dinner. All Taliya needed to do was take care of herself. She eyed the surviving choices on the buffet tables. Many platters were empty, with only colorful crumbs left behind carrying the scent of curry and spices. Kano whuffed in dismay.

"It's not unusual," Grampa Jai said, handing her a plate. "I've read many stories about the bride and groom not getting to eat a bite."

Marla sidled up to Taliya, adjusted the dupatta around the bride's shoulders, then leaned in conspiratorially. "My gulab jamun is hiding in the car. We can pull it out later, when the crowd thins. And there's leftover barbeque in the fridge."

Taliya made a few selections, but she stopped at one that was different from the rest. The scent of it had been lingering around the compound for hours. No spices. Very beige. Carl's offering.

"He says it's called funeral potatoes," Shreya said, spooning some up from the self-warming pot and adding it to Taliya's plate. "What the grandmothers of his family have brought to every potluck event for generations, not just funerals."

"Humans and their casseroles," Kano said with a chuckle. "I smell onions and cheese."

"There's actually two cans of thick soup in there," Shreya said, wrinkling her nose.

Taliya realized it was one of the few barely touched dishes and added another serving to her plate before Carl noticed.

Marla led them to an empty table Aliania had set aside for the wedding party, and they ate while watching neighbors visit with hugs and animated conversations. The whole potluck situation seemed to have worked out just fine, even if her choices had been limited. There was more than enough food. She noticed some guests going back for seconds and suspected nothing would be left in the end.

Some items were familiar, but many must be family favorites because she'd never tasted anything like them. While there were a few Indian-style dishes, most felt more like local traditions or American food. Or maybe those were the dishes still left. Meatballs in barbeque sauce. Mini quiches. Something her father called "pigs in blankets." Even chocolate cupcakes with thick frosting, evidence of which could only be found now around the sticky mouths of the kits. Maybe tigran were developing an appreciation for sweets. Carl's potatoes were interesting, but Taliya wouldn't be requesting the recipe.

Tuscan and Tyler swung by with glasses of ale for each of them, and she suspected the party was about to get going. A clinking sound drew her attention to Carl, now standing at the end of their table. Taliya noticed some swaying and wondered how deep the general was in the ale. All of the guests joined in, tapping their glasses with silverware or a claw.

"I have been nominated," he said, bringing the clinking to an end, "to provide the official toast at these nuptials." He raised his glass and turned to Taliya and Kano. "My friends, may your love grow stronger with every passing year. May your home be filled with joy. May your journey through life together be filled with mutual understanding, loyal support, and great adventures. And may your undying love see you through all of it. To Taliya and Kano!"

"To Taliya and Kano!" the guest shouted, then cheered and clapped when the pair kissed, like they were expected to.

"That sounds like a perfect future," Kano whispered to Taliya.

"It does." She flared her whiskers. "Though I could do without any more great adventures."

Music with deep bass rhythms and Indian-style drumming that vibrated through the ground began, and the reception shifted into the next phase. The dozens of kits on hand rushed to the dance floor—though it was just matted-down grass in the center of the canopy. The grown-ups finished their meals while the young ones flailed around and stomped to the beat, stirring up the scent of the marigold petals scattered on the lawn. Amrita and Disha held hands and spun each other round and round until they collapsed in the grass. Then jumped up and did it again.

As the music shifted into a similar rhythmic song, a few adults set aside their empty plates to join the dancing, and Taliya considered it. In the snug, fancy sari, wiggling was the most she'd be able to pull off.

"We have to dance." Kano stood and held out his hand. "It's only polite."

Taliya snorted but took it and let him lead her to the middle of the canopy, garnering excited cheers from the crowd. While she did her best at some finger-tutting and hip-swirling, Kano relished the chance to show off his exceptional skills at Indian-style dance and encouraged the adults to join in.

Soon nearly every guest had joined the sea of color gyrating and jumping under the canopy. Even Samson allowed himself to be dragged onto the floor by a female tigran who made sparkly eyes at him while her friends watched wistfully, maybe regretting not being as bold themselves.

Partway through the song, Kano pointed out that Aliania was dancing with three tigran males her age, all strutting their best moves while she seemed oblivious, swiveling and tutting in her own world. Her father shook his head and grumbled, but Taliya was sure he'd made note of exactly who those future suitors were. How Ali would ever be able to date, for a number of reasons, was a battle for another day. Hopefully another year.

After two more songs, Taliya begged her way off the dance floor and got some ale from her father, who was serving as bartender. A quieter slow-dance song began, and Kano swayed with all three of his kits—Ali at his waist and a twin around each leg.

Taliya spotted the new family of cheeman hovering off to the side near her parents' house, looking uncomfortable either with so many excited creatures or with being the only of their species there. Their overall appearance was like a liran, but their faces had the distinctive ebony cheetah lines from the inside corner of their eyes to their chins, with a freckling of black dots, while quarter-sized dots were visible on their arms. They were dressed in multi-colored African-style tunics and slacks, celebrating that portion of their DNA, and open-toed sandals. Taliya suspected non-retractable claws made any other footwear nearly impossible.

Oddly, the family hadn't come through the greeting line after the ceremony, so she skirted around the edge of the canopy to welcome them in the lull between loud songs. Seeing her approach, they all smiled, but she could smell their anxiety.

"I'm so glad you could join us," Taliya said, making pointed eye contact with both adults and then all five kits, who appeared to be between six and four years old— maybe a set of twins and a set of triplets, based on their size. "And welcome to the community. You moved in about three weeks ago now, right?"

The female nodded and seemed to relax a bit. "The property was donated to us by a family after their elderly parents died. So generous."

"We thought we'd be at the camp forever," the male

said. "But it was better than the breeding facility, so we hated to complain."

Taliya whuffed. "The one in Colorado? We were there too."

"I remember seeing you two, during the escape." The female tipped her head and smiled. "Your husband stands out a bit."

The raucous music started up again, and Taliya realized more conversation was going to be tricky above the noise. "I have your contact information now," she shouted. "Let's get the kits together soon."

The five young ones all grinned, revealing their tiny fangs, and the adults nodded their approval—purrs emanating from all of them.

"Taliya!"

She turned to watch Carl dancing toward them, military jacket open and flapping, doing some kind of cha-cha, fingers snapping above his head. When he reached her, she found herself wrapped up in an ale-scented embrace.

"Maaan, I love ya, Taliya," Carl mumbled into the gold jewelry around her neck. "I'm so happy for you two!" He leaned back and made glassy-eyed contact. "This is the best wedding ever."

Taliya laughed and pushed him upright by the shoulders. "I love you too, Carl. And I guess you're enjoying Papa's ale."

He threw back his head with a howl, drawing the attention of guests around them and giggles from the cheeman kits. Aliania appeared, and Carl howled again at the sight of her before squashing her to his chest.

"You put together an amazing party," he gushed. "You're the best. The very, very best."

Ali shifted her face to avoid his medals poking her in the eye. "Thanks."

Carl released her and boogied off into the crowd with moves that were downright old-time disco.

"I *love* Drunk Uncle Carl!" Aliania shouted over the music with a grin.

Carl spun and hit a pose with one hand pointing at the sky. "I love you two, my little marshmallow!"

The general grabbed up his mate, and the pair began sort of slow dancing while Rey laughed, probably teasing him about how drunk he was. A perfect moment showcasing their victory over the cruelty and hatred that had kept them apart.

Aliania grinned. "Never seen him so relaxed and happy."

While Taliya had memories of jovial, day-off tipsy Carl the refugee camp soldier, it had been years since she'd witnessed that side of him. Ali had been too young to really remember Carl before Reynaldo was kidnapped and his focus was constantly on that rescue. Often angry and frustrated. Always worried and a bit reserved, though Taliya's brothers and her kits usually brought him out of that temporarily. He could play and be silly with them, but part of him was always on alert to rush off and save Rey at a moment's notice. A goal he'd only accomplished a couple of weeks ago. If Carl wanted to get sloppy drunk and dance until he collapsed at her wedding, he was welcome to it.

And Rey . . . As far as Taliya was concerned, Rey could do whatever the hell he wanted for the rest of his life. She caught his eye over Carl's shoulder, and he slow-blinked, which she returned with a smile.

Taliya turned back to the cheeman family, but they'd moved on toward the transports, probably heading home. Samson would know their names, which she'd neglected to ask. Kano pulled her back onto the dance floor before she could worry too much more about it.

The sun was beginning to set, and the crowd had thinned significantly. Her parents settled on the porch with the dogs—now free of the elephant costumes— while Tuscan and Tyler were intent on charming two females their age across the lawn. About twenty younger tigran still enjoyed the dance floor, but the only kits remaining were Taliya's. Kano had removed his jacket, and the atmosphere felt more relaxed.

She caught Aliania's gaze and pointed at her shoes, still obediently on her feet. Ali laughed and shook her head before sticking out her own bare foot.

"Traitor!" Taliya immediately kicked her own shoes under a table with great gusto. She wished there was a plan for her to change clothes, but that would have to wait until the guests all headed home. She could play the bride for another few hours. Then she'd be grateful to remove the heavy necklace and bracelets, along with the binding sari, and party on the lawn in her PJs.

Marla danced out of the main house balancing the reserved platter of gulab jamun, Amrita and Little Jai right at her heels.

"Your parents get first choice!" Marla shouted, not discouraging their jumps at the treats one bit.

She reached Taliya and Kano and offered up the tray of fried dough balls in syrup with tiny bamboo toothpicks in them to avoid sticky fingers and fur. Taliya popped one in her mouth and relished the warm, soft-as-butter dough that was just a bit sweet, with cardamom, a touch of rose, and a hint of saffron.

"Marla, they're perfect!" Taliya said before taking two more. She hesitated, feeling guilty for a second, then remembered it was her damn wedding.

"There's another tray," Marla said with a proud grin. "Eat all you want."

The kits squealed and jumped up and down at that suggestion. Marla lowered the tray, and they each grabbed a handful and dashed away, screaming with delight and dripping syrup on the lawn.

"Wash your hands when you're done!" Taliya called after them.

Kano took two for himself before Marla headed into the remaining crowd, who welcomed the dessert with hoots and cheers. Taliya smiled, noticing her friend's fancy hairdo had definitely not survived the dancing, long dark locks now hanging down her back.

Kano took the toothpicks from Taliya, tossed them in the garbage, and wrapped her up in his arms, despite the fast rhythms currently playing. She rested her head on his chest and sighed, glad they were far away from the blasting speakers but nice and close to the cool blowers.

As they swayed peacefully, Taliya spotted Joe, still taking pictures. He'd captured so many moments she looked forward to sorting through. A drone swooped eye-level with them, and the couple waved at it.

"Good night, Madame President," Taliya said. "Thank you for coming. Sorry you couldn't enjoy the food."

The drone tipped sideways in what felt like a wink, then whooshed off to land on the porch with the others, where Samson could collect them later. The dogs eyed it but didn't move from Shreya's side.

"So," Kano said, "what changes, now that I'm lawfully your husband?"

"You're stuck with me *forever* now."

He pressed his forehead against hers. "That was already true. Wild bears couldn't tear me away."

"Aww." She kissed him, chuffed gently, and bopped his leg with her tail. "Me neither. So nothing else changes, really. But Ali will be satisfied."

"For today, at least."

Taliya chuckled. "And I suppose we have proven a point to the government. Creatures do want this, officially and legally."

"Only logical that you'd be the tigran to represent that."

"Maybe some other creature can take the lead next time."

He met her gaze with a half smile, and she flared her whiskers.

"Yeah, yeah." She chuckled. "Probably not. But for tonight, let's just enjoy all of this. Our home. Family. Friends. All of it."

He pulled away, took her by the hand, and gently spun her in a circle. "That sounds perfect, my lovely wife."

"Perfect *forever*, my magnificent husband."

Taliya
and the
Uncivilized

CHAPTER 1
NOVEMBER 2176

Taliya ducked under another low branch and stepped hesitantly over a massive fallen log. Kano grabbed her elbow, maybe sensing she was losing her balance. He wasn't wrong, but her tension had more to do with who they were looking for, not the undergrowth. They'd been hiking for miles through the dense Colorado forest, and she was grateful she'd worn sturdy hiking boots and heavier clothes than the normal tunic and slacks in her wardrobe. The thick pants had already protected her from more than one stab of a broken branch. A few trees here and there were losing their multi-colored leaves, and the air held a comfortable chill—giving a hint of the snow a few weeks away.

Mountains rose up on both sides along the wildlife trail they were following to avoid climbing as much as possible. It was overgrown and not the most direct route to the coordinates on the map but saved energy. The smells of pine, urine markings from various wild animals, and decaying leaves swirled around them in a comfortable blend of nature. A mountain lion had passed along the route recently, but Taliya felt confident the cat wasn't currently in the area. An ancient maple tree nearby reeked of bear. One had probably rubbed his back all over it. Hopefully, he was foraging elsewhere too.

She paused and took a swig from the metal canteen hooked to her waistband. Kano followed her lead, and their eyes met—golden and blue in the shadowy woods. It was unusual for them to be alone together without a kit demanding attention. She slow-blinked at her husband, and he chuffed gently. Taliya doubted the next few weeks would be as peaceful as the last two days of traveling. Kano pulled the GPS device from his pocket and checked their location.

"It shouldn't be far now," he said, "based on the information we have."

After their trip to Geneva and the United Nations, President Padme Nakobi had contacted Taliya about a group of tigran who were living wild in the forests of Colorado. There had been reports of missing livestock in the area, and the ranchers and farmers were blaming these tigran. Some borders were in place, mostly because the tigran were living on government-owned land, but the humans claimed the tigran were hunting on their land, taking from their herds.

Since tigran were now an endangered species, avoiding conflict between the creatures and the ranchers was vital. The president had entrusted Taliya to go and meet with the "uncivilized" tigran in the forest to try and find some answers—and hopefully a solution to the human's complaints.

It was nice to be so trusted—to be the go-to tigran for the president of the United States—but some days Taliya wished she'd never gotten involved in politics. It wasn't something she'd aimed for. The international news outlets had glommed onto the story of her kidnapping from the refugee camp, and the die was cast.

The slight breeze among the trees shifted and brought Taliya a distinctive familiar odor. Kano stiffened, on full alert.

"If we can smell *them* . . ." he said.

She nodded. The group of wild tigran surely knew they were there.

Reclipping her canteen, she scanned the area, her sensitive ears twisting and turning. Kano sorted out the scents around them, snuffling and turning in a slow circle. He stopped, facing the way they had been heading.

"There," he said. "They're up ahead."

Moving cautiously, the pair started again, chuffing a greeting of peace every few steps.

Taliya had never met an uncivilized tigran. Those who were caught in the Gathering were usually executed on the spot. She wished they'd brought some reinforcements, but the plan was to greet the group without any show of weapons or force. From reports of missing troops in the area during the war, the army suspected the tigran were quick to terminate any humans who trespassed into their territory. Taliya hoped their animosity was directed only at humans, not all interlopers.

The smell of tigran had grown stronger, but Taliya sensed it was more than just up ahead. Kano hesitated and put a hand out to stop her. He chuffed and lifted his arms to show he wasn't carrying a weapon. Taliya did the same. She hoped the wild tigran couldn't smell the guns in their backpacks.

"We're surrounded," Kano whispered. "Some of them have circled around behind us."

Taliya's tail puffed involuntarily, and her hackles spiked all along her back. She tried to chuff again, but it came out weakly, more like a human raspberry blert. *So much for not showing fear.* Kano appeared to be staying cooler. As a massive male, he'd really have to keep himself under control and not appear threatening in any way. She cleared her throat and stood straight, still keeping her arms up a bit, showing that her hands were empty.

"My name is Taliya Sharma. There's nothing to fear from us."

A low grumbled laugh emanated from her right, close to the ground. Maybe behind a fallen tree.

"Why would we fear you, tame little tigran?" a male voice said. "We are not the ones lost in the woods."

As they both turned in the direction of the voice, the head of a gigantic tigran lifted above a log and met their eyes. She felt a wave of shock from Kano and tried to control her own reaction. No one had mentioned how huge these creatures were. Or was it just the one greeting them?

"We're not lost," she managed to say. "My mate and I are looking for you."

"Take your pale mate," the tigran said, "and walk forward until you reach the lake. We will follow."

Taliya swallowed firmly, wondering how many "we" involved. The report had been of a dozen uncivilized tigran. What if there were more? In all reality, it would only take a couple to be a danger to them. She turned to meet Kano's eyes, and he nodded sharply and pointed the way. She could smell a large source of fresh water in that direction. Taliya started forward, Kano close behind her, protective.

After traveling for a few minutes, Taliya spotted the water up ahead. They stepped out of the forest and stood in awe at the beauty of the scene. The lake sprawled across a large valley, with towering snowcapped mountains reflected in the water. It looked like a picture postcard for the wilderness of Colorado. Along the shoreline were remnants of what must have been cabins and tourist lodging, but it was all dilapidated and unused now. Some of them were even surrounded by water—looking like collapsed house boats—proving the lake was much larger now than in the campsite's heyday. It was rare to run across leftovers from the past. Most were bulldozed and replaced. Here in the wilderness, no one had bothered.

Next to her, Kano sighed. "The group certainly picked an amazing spot for their camp."

They both turned as the tigran who had greeted them stepped out of the tree line about twenty yards away.

"I am Severo, lead male for this clan."

Taliya stared up at his golden eyes, trying to contain her emotions. Severo was over eight feet tall, a full head above Kano, plus heavier by many pounds of toned muscle.

And he didn't have on a stitch of clothing.

She should have expected it. That was part of the whole "uncivilized" thing, but it was still shocking. At least his fur was long enough to cover most of the area she was valiantly trying to avert her eyes from.

Kano breathed slowly and carefully beside her, keeping his responses in check. Aside from Samson the ligran and the huge berman, it was rare Kano was outmatched by any creature. Instinctive reactions were hard to control, and there was a whole ocean of testosterone emanating from Severo.

Another tigran stepped out of the forest and stood next to him. She was smaller but still the largest female tigran Taliya had ever seen—nearly as big as Kano. She was naked as well, but also mostly covered by fur that was long and thick. Probably from living outdoors in the Colorado winters.

"I am Jacy, Severo's mate," she said, moving to stand slightly in front of him.

Taliya had no idea what etiquette the situation required. Padme had often briefed her on cultural differences before she met the dignitaries of other countries.

Even as a tigran, she wanted to be respectful of human expectations. But no one except the uncivilized tigran knew their rules. Kano didn't budge, and she realized he was expecting her to take the lead. She was the one who'd been sent by the president, after all.

"I'm Taliya," she said, copying their first-name-only style. *Do they have last names?* "And this is my mate, Kano."

"I have never seen a white tigran before," Jacy said, scanning Kano up and down. "I'm afraid you wouldn't last long trying to hunt in the woods. No camouflage at all."

"White tigran are something created by humans, not something nature designed or approved," Kano said with a half smile.

"Well, aren't we all," Severo said dryly.

There was a rustling in the undergrowth nearby, and Taliya spotted bits of orange through the trees. *Is the rest of the group hiding? Waiting to attack?*

"We're sorry for trespassing and disturbing your peace," Taliya said. "I was sent by President Nakobi. I serve as the tigran representative to the government."

Severo and Jacy exchanged a look, and she chuffed at him in way that sounded sad.

"Does this president plan to move us from our land?" Severo asked, the black lines on his face shifting into a frown.

"Absolutely not," Taliya said. "We're hoping to establish a safe zone for your group, but there are concerns about possible overlaps with some nearby human territory. Livestock deaths reported by the farmers and ranchers who live on the outskirts. We need to confirm some land borders."

"We do not hunt cows or anything from the ranches or farmland," Severo said firmly.

Jacy nodded. "But we have information about those attacks that you may find interesting."

Before Taliya could ask for details, Severo whuffed, and this was apparently the "all clear" signal. The tiny heads of several kits popped up from behind the bushes. They scampered out to join the four tigran. With the arrival of the kits, Taliya felt the atmosphere around them shift. Severo had decided they were not a threat and was accepting them as visitors.

"We call ourselves the Nuche Clan," Severo said, "because our territory meets the Ute Reservation here in the mountains. Humans call them Ute, but they call themselves Nuche, or mountain people. They are the only humans we interact with."

Taliya nodded and smiled at the four little tigran of varying sizes, three of whom clustered tightly around Jacy's legs. She leaned over to be on their eye level.

"Hello."

The kits stared back at her with wide eyes. One pointed at her boots and giggled.

"Do you have kits?" Jacy asked.

"Yes," Taliya said. "Kano and I have twins of our own and a daughter from his first marriage. Before the Gathering."

Jacy tipped her head in acknowledged sadness. Apparently, no one needed to explain what had happened to that first wife, even here in the wilderness.

"Are they white or orange?" Severo asked as one of the littlest kits moved over to hang on his tail.

Kano answered this time. "Our older daughter is pure white. Of the twins, one is orange and the other is strawberry."

"Strawberry?" Jacy said with a frown.

"A rare side effect of the white mutation," Kano said. "White fur, like mine, but with pale orange stripes. Humans get very excited about it."

"Humans often value what looks interesting over what is useful," Severo said.

I doubt he knows the half of how true that is.

"Come," Jacy said. "Share a meal with us, and we will tell you what we know about the killing of tame animals."

The kits all vanished into the woods again, giggling amongst themselves and leaving the four adults alone for their discussion. Jacy headed off down the shoreline, and the three other tigran followed her. Faint tracks of what were once roads indicated this had been a popular spot a century or so ago. About fifty yards away, there was a clearing on the beach with logs arranged in a seating area around a campfire.

Taliya glanced over at Kano, and he raised one stripe of an eyebrow. They hadn't expected to see fire being used. Taliya wondered what other assumptions about uncivilized tigran were wrong. Waiting diplomatically to see who took which spots, Taliya and Kano only sat after Jacy indicated a place for them next to her. They set down their backpacks and canteens and joined the couple on a log.

"We won't need the fire tonight," Severo said, "except maybe for dinner, but it still serves as a meeting area."

"There are many things we don't know about how you live," Taliya said. "I have to admit, the campfire surprised me."

She hoped she hadn't offended them, but neither reacted.

"Fire is necessary here in the mountains," Jacy said. "Our human genetics make us weaker than we should be. But once the snow and winter truly set in, we mostly stick to the caves and stay out of the worst of the weather."

Caves? They live in caves? Taliya wished she'd brought something to write on, but she wasn't sure how the clan would feel about being studied. Jacy seemed to read her thoughts.

"We don't live like wild animals, you know," she said with a smile.

"No, I guess I really don't," Taliya admitted. "I've heard stories and rumors over the years, but the world at large knows very little about you. And I'll admit, that could make it tricky to secure this land for your clan. It's hard to get humans interested in things they don't understand and appreciate."

"Maybe if we were all *white* tigran," Severo said with a snort.

"Oh no," Kano said, "that would be much worse. Then you'd have financial value. A commodity to be bought and sold. Much better to be under the radar than coveted for the color of your fur."

"It had been a blessing," Severo said, "being able to stay hidden for decades, but the end of that began when the Army arrived."

"We lost so many from our clan during the Gathering," Jacy said. "The Enforcers never even tried to capture us. Hundreds were simply murdered and left to rot where they dropped."

Taliya's skin prickled at imagined images of that scene. Kano shifted next to her, knowing all too well what it felt like to watch those you love be senselessly murdered. Taliya chuffed comfortingly at him and wrapped an arm around his waist.

"Those were dark days for all of us," she said. "I'm always thankful for the humans who supported the tigran or at least hated Kerkaw enough to battle against him as well."

"Have they found him yet?" Jacy asked. "Last we heard from the Nuche, he had escaped justice of any kind."

"No," Kano said. "He's still out there. There are humans who shelter and protect him. I'm not sure I'll rest completely at ease as long as he roams the earth."

The other three nodded and then were silent for a moment, quiet with their own fears and memories.

"We hope you'll stay with us for a while," Jacy finally said. "If you can share with your president what our lives are actually like, she will realize the animals being killed have nothing to do with our clan."

"It would be an honor," Taliya said. "We want very much to understand how you live and how much space you need to do that comfortably."

That was already part of the plan: visit and learn what they could. Aunty Marla was prepared to stay with the kits for the next month, if necessary, on the Arkansas compound. Having Taliya's parents—Shreya and Grampa Jai—living in their cottage across the meadow was helpful, but the kits were a bit much for them 24/7. The twins were a handful on a good day.

"My hope is to get the government to protect this land for you," Taliya continued, "rather like the reservation the Nuche have, so you can be free to live as you please."

"That would be wonderful," Jacy said. "We have dreaded humans showing up to claim this land. The Nuche have shared their history, how other humans forced them off their land, little by little, until they only had the reservation left. They warned us this day would come."

"No one is going to force you to leave," Taliya said.

She hoped with all her heart that stayed true.

———◦◦◦———

AFTER A MEAL OF FRESH VENISON——RAW, WHICH WAS A FIRST FOR Taliya and Kano and sat hard in their stomachs—Jacy gave the pair a brief tour of the area around the lake and a clearing in the woods that served as their camp. They were introduced to dozens of tigran. All enormous. All extra furry and naked as the day they were born. There were twenty-two family groupings, each with their own area and firepit. Beds were made from leaves and evergreen branches with animal hides as blankets. After the tour, Severo and Kano wandered off, talking about hunting and tanning hides for winter, while Taliya and Jacy stayed closer to camp.

In one area, a mother cuddled a young kit, maybe a year old, and groomed her with long licks of her rough tongue. Taliya caught herself staring. How would it feel to groom her own kits that way? Jacy seemed confused by Taliya's interest in a simple bath, so Taliya stuck out her bare, human-like tongue and smiled. Jacy stuck out her own tongue, covered in feline spikes, and smiled back.

"I've heard some tigran have tongues like you," Jacy said. "We all have true tiger tongues. Maybe it's something in our bloodlines."

"Were you ever in a facility?" Taliya asked.

"Oh no. We've been living free for several generations. I remember the stories my great-grandparents told around the fire during the long winters, about the first creation of the tigran and being released from the labs to help humans rebuild their society. Most tigran who live wild, like us, rebelled from day one. We never understood why we had to work for the human population and ran off the first chance we got. Clans slowly formed. We took to the forests and secluded places where humans didn't live.

It was only when the Gathering began that they paid any attention to us."

Jacy hesitated, and Taliya felt a wave of sadness from her. She sat down on a nearby stump, and Taliya sat on another across from her, sensing that something more needed to be shared. Finally, Jacy cleared her throat and met Taliya's eyes.

"We didn't have any warning. Knew nothing about the Gathering. The forest was just suddenly full of men hunting us. Enforcers arrived and started shooting." She hesitated and looked out at the water. "Even the kits. No one they found was spared. The woods are dense, so many of us were able to hide. Friends from the Nuche Reservation arrived the next day to warn us, but it was too late by then."

Taliya laid her ears back, able to vividly imagine the terror of those hiding while their friends and family were slaughtered. It was the kind of nightmare she'd had many times while she was secreted in the warehouse attic, and even afterward, at the breeding facility and the refugee camp. Sometimes even now, in her safe Arkansas home.

"The Nuche helped us gather the dead," Jacy said. "Normally, we burn those who have died and scatter the ashes, but we were terrified to light fires. We buried the bodies ten at a time. There were more than a dozen graves that day."

Taliya gritted her teeth with a snort. *Such a waste! Such a hate-filled, pointless waste of life.*

"Those of us who remained took refuge in our cave

system. It is very well hidden, and we hoped that by staying out of sight the Enforcers would think we had been eliminated. We hunted at night and avoided fires. That was a long few months. A very cold winter. Until the Nuche leaders arrived to let us know the war was over and it was safe to live in the open again."

"It is safe," Taliya assured her, "for the most part, at least. Humans are always unpredictable."

"How did you come to work for the president of the United States?" Jacy asked, leaning on a tree behind her. "It seems an odd job for a tigran, even after the war."

Taliya smiled. "That is a very long and complicated story, maybe better for a quiet evening around the campfire."

"I look forward to it," Jacy said. "We rarely hear stories about the outside world. Once you start sharing your adventures, the young ones may never stop begging you for more."

"Then it's a good thing Kano and I will be here for a while. I'm happy to answer any of their questions. There are many sad and strange steps that led us to where we are now. I certainly never would have imagined the life I have. Not in a million years."

Kano and Severo rejoined them, returning from their separate tour and conversation in the woods. Manly stuff, Taliya assumed. More about hunting, maybe. Kano would give her the details later.

"Taliya and I were just discussing how she came to

work for the government," Jacy said. "And how the world is safer for tigran now."

"Humans will always be humans, though," Taliya said. "Kano and I still fear for our unique kits, who have immense financial value. People have done horrible things trying to get their hands on them." Her canines ached at the memory of a sharp metal object being jammed into their nerves. Torture to force her to turn over the girls. She shook her head gently. "I'm not sure those battles will ever end, even once they're grown."

"We do not feel fully at peace either," Severo said. "We hope you will understand when we don't show you the hidden caves."

Taliya held up a hand. "I completely understand. I mean, I would love to see how you survive the brutal winters here, but I respect your very well-founded concerns. Hopefully, we can officially secure this whole area for you. We just need to determine the boundaries and clear things up with the ranchers."

Severo and Jacy exchanged a look, and Kano gave a frustrated huff.

"Severo has explained some things to me," he said. "About the livestock problems."

"Oh?" Taliya glanced back and forth among the three of them. "Do you know who's attacking the farms and the animals?"

"Yes," Severo said, "in a way. We believe *no one* is attacking them. They complained to the Nuche, who then told us about their claims we were hunting on their property. The farmers and ranchers want to expand and take more of the land for themselves. We are in their way, and they fear us enough to be worried about just trying to push us out."

Taliya asked with wide eyes, "Are you saying the humans are making up stories about attacks so they can place the blame on you? Get you relocated or removed?"

"Does that sound unlike human behavior to you?" Jacy asked.

"No," Taliya admitted with a sigh. "It sounds *exactly* like human behavior."

"But we'll have to find a way to prove it," Kano said, ears back. "You know how this will go in Congress if we can't. Blah, blah, blah, next. No protection. No reservation."

Taliya nodded sadly. Then she thought of the security system they had in place around the Arkansas compound at home. Couldn't cameras come in handy to prove the tigran were innocent? She looked into the trees, trying to imagine what kind of arrangement they could rig. Kano seemed to follow her reasoning.

"Would you allow us to place some wildlife cameras along the area between your land and the farmers and ranchers?" Kano asked.

He explained the system his own family used for security and described how it could be applied at the territory border—without revealing anything about the tigran clan's life deeper in the forest.

"We would have to be careful," Taliya said, "and make

sure the humans in question don't know about it. Then, when they make a claim against you, we would have proof that no tigran had crossed the border."

Severo and Jacy appeared skeptical—frowns etched deeply into the black lines of their faces—and Taliya didn't blame them. Living the way they chose to, technology of any kind would be foreign and suspect. Allowing surveillance cameras to be rigged up in their territory might well feel like the first step in government oversight of their lives.

"It would only be temporary," Taliya assured them. "Once this issue is over, we will make sure it is all removed."

"You will find that the humans trespass onto our land, not the other way around," Jacy said with a growl in her throat.

"If I didn't believe that," Taliya said, "I would never suggest this solution. I fully expect it will help resolve the accusations."

Jacy nodded sharply, still looking concerned. "We should discuss this with the clan."

"Of course," Taliya said. "How about Kano and I go back to the campfire area so you can have privacy to consider the next steps? I need to touch base with President Nakobi anyhow and let her know we've made contact and a plan is formulating."

"You trust this President Nakobi?" Severo asked.

"Yes," Taliya said. "She has a good heart, is a strong

supporter of tigran rights, and really does want to help. That's always a solid place to start."

<hr>

AFTER SENDING A TEXTED REPORT TO THE PRESIDENT, TALIYA tucked her communicator back into her pocket and gazed up at the mountains. There was something magical about their stature, especially as the images reflected back into the water of the lake. Many features of the landscape reminded her of home, but Arkansas mountains were nothing like Colorado mountains—more like wimpy rolling hills in comparison. A bald eagle soared over the water, hunting for dinner like she'd seen them do over Beaver Lake near the homestead, but somehow even this eagle seemed larger and more impressive than its Arkansas cousins.

A memory hit her from the first days at the breeding facility—of the elevator door opening as she emerged from the dungeon to reveal similar woods and mountains and smells of oncoming winter. She shook her head to dislodge the memory of fear and replaced it with meeting Kano that day as well. She'd had no clue about the new future for her life that would initiate.

He stretched out on the sand and rested his head on a small log, eyes closed. She sat down on the log next to him.

"It smells like Christmas," he murmured.

She chuckled and inhaled deeply, enjoying the evergreen trees and fresh outdoor air. Birds twittered in the forest, and a hungry woodpecker rapped on a tree nearby. It was lovely to have an assignment that let her be in nature instead of stuck in an airplane or office somewhere.

"So are the ranchers flat-out lying?" she asked. "Are they harming their cattle to set up the tigran?"

"If the clan agrees to the cameras, we'll have an answer soon. Do you suppose the Nuche can help vouch for the tigran here? They would be having the same problems as the ranchers if the tigran were really hunting outside of their territory."

"From what I've witnessed, different types of humans don't trust each other much. I'm not sure Congress would listen to the Nuche over the ranchers, who are very adamant about the tigran attacks."

"They won't like being proved wrong," Kano said. "Especially if we can show they are blatantly lying and setting things up to look bad for the tigran. Being wrong is one thing. Intentionally trying to frame a creature is something else entirely."

From what Taliya had learned over the last two years, humans definitely did not like to be revealed as liars, no matter how clearly the lie could be proven. Even if she could reveal evidence that the farmers and ranchers were conspiring against Severo's clan, would Congress accept it and act in favor of the tigran and their territory? Or would the humans win anyhow, like so many times before over so many generations? Was the whole trip a big waste of time and energy? She needed to establish something for these tigran that could outlive President Nakobi's time in office. Taliya's tail puffed and thrashed behind her on the log.

Kano opened one blue eye and looked at her.

"You can only do so much here, Taliya. Don't take the whole weight and responsibility of their lives onto your striped shoulders."

"I know. I know."

He sat up and stared out at the lake before standing and undressing. Taliya watched for a minute and then laughed.

"What're you doing?"

"Going for a swim," Kano said. "I highly recommend you join me."

Taliya glanced back at the woods, wondering how long it would be until the meeting was over.

"They're already naked, Taliya," he said with a laugh. "I don't think you being without clothes is going to shock them. It might even make them feel more comfortable."

Taliya chuckled. He was probably right. But she wasn't just brought up to be civilized. She was brought up *super*-civilized. She'd never stepped outside of her house naked in her life. But she had been skinny-dipping. Many times. The neighbors had a lake on their property. Taliya had joined them for dozens of splashes over the years.

While she pondered that, Kano kicked off his boots, dropped his britches, and strode into the lake in all his muscular black-and-white glory. That was something even better to ponder. She watched until he was submerged and swimming gracefully deeper into the lake, alternating between the breast stroke and freestyle crawl.

With a snort she stood, stripped, and joined him. *Which is the odder state of things, really? Half-tiger creatures who wear clothes or half-tiger creatures who don't?*

The fall air blew crisply through her fur, and she reveled in the feeling. Kano turned to watch her appreciatively as she stepped from the sandy shore into the rockier bed of the lake. The water was cold, but it felt invigorating. Splashing her way deeper, she quickly reached a point where she lifted off and floated. Kano swam to meet her and wrapped his arms around her, pulling her back to where they could just stand with their heads above water. She curled her tail around his leg and snuggled in close to his warmth.

"Now this is a lovely way to spend the afternoon," he said. "No politics or phone calls or humans of any kind."

Taliya kissed him and then lay her head back in the water, floating slightly and gazing up at the bright blue sky. She relaxed into the moment, trying to let her worries wash away. Kano's hands drifted lower on her back, and he rumbled deep in his throat. She lifted her head and met his eyes, sensing his interest had shifted.

"In the middle of a lake?" She chuffed in amusement.

"Why not?"

"Because we're here as representatives of the government, not on holiday, you silly male. Have some self-control."

"We should have thought about that before we started the whole naked-with-no-kits-around thing."

Taliya laughed and pushed him away. "There are certainly kits around, just not ours. For all we know, they're watching us right now. More swimming. Less whatever else."

Kano laughed and dove under the water. She felt him swim past her leg, then he popped up ten yards away.

"Maybe I can catch something for dinner and help contribute to our visit," he said.

After diving and flopping around in the water while Taliya floated contentedly nearby, Kano caught two large bass and was immensely proud of himself. The pair splashed back to shore, shook off most of the water, and air-dried while Kano gave his prize fish a quick gutting with his pocket knife and then rinsed his hands in the lake.

"I hope they let us *cook* it," Taliya said.

"No sushi?"

"I don't think you're supposed to do that with fresh-water fish."

"Look who's the cooking expert," Kano said, laughing as he pulled his pants back on over sandy furry feet.

"I don't even know how I know that," Taliya admitted. "One of those old cooking competition shows on TV, maybe."

She considered not getting dressed again, but the thought of Severo returning to find her clad in nothing but her fur made her flush with embarrassment. Better to stay formal for this visit.

Kano chuffed as she put her clothes back on. "So civilized," he teased.

"You've got your pants on, I notice."

"Yes. We are both far too civilized. We should have naked days at home."

"The kits would love that," she admitted. "A little bit of wildness never hurt anyone."

Severo and Jacy emerged from the trees, and Taliya and Kano rose to meet them.

"The clan has agreed to the cameras," Severo said. "As long as they are kept only near the borders and do not record our daily life."

"Excellent," Taliya said. "I'll contact the president and arrange for them to be installed immediately. I'll oversee the whole thing."

"Is anyone speaking to the ranchers about this?" Jacy said. "Asking them to prove *their* claims?"

"The government is listening to their complaints," Taliya said, "but they don't know we are here. Only a handful of people do. We want the ranchers to continue with whatever has been going on and not know they're being watched, though I doubt it would occur to them we'd rig up cameras."

Taliya took out her com to communicate everything to President Nakobi, while Kano proudly presented his fishy conquests to the tigran. Severo assured him they would all enjoy the fish for dinner—cooked. Before Taliya finished her message, Jacy had started a campfire with a piece of flint and a knife.

At the smell of burning wood, the rest of the clan began to gather. Taliya realized she was going to have to learn some names quickly. Two teenage-looking tigran ran and splashed into the lake, probably to snag a few more fish. There were a lot of mouths to feed on a daily basis, living only off the land.

A response popped up on her screen that two technicians would arrive in the morning at a set of coordinates along the border to rig up the cameras. She acknowledged that she would meet them there, then put away her device to enjoy the evening. If all went according to her own personal plan, she and Kano would sleep out here by the lake, under the stars.

CHAPTER 2

A sharp whistle sounded from her left, and Taliya twisted an ear in that direction. The sun was barely up, but she was in place to meet the security technicians right at the northern end of the border between the government land where the tigran lived and the ranchers' territory. Kano and Severo waited out of sight in the woods behind her so the clan leader could witness the process but not be seen.

The sound of leaves crunching under boots led her directly to the two technicians. When she was close, Taliya chuffed to get their attention. She'd never been any good at whistling. Most tigran weren't. The pair nodded to her and motioned to follow them.

Using a GPS system, they determined where the edge of the northern-most rancher's land began. Beyond that line was more national forest.

"Our supervisor mentioned you have this system at home," one of them said.

"Yes. We've had trouble with humans wanting to steal our kits."

The look of first surprise and then outrage on the man's face suggested he would be supportive of the tigran here in the forest.

"These cameras are activated by motion sensors," he continued, still frowning, "basically wildlife tracking for their general use. If anyone or any animal comes within range, it will record their movements."

"That should meet our needs perfectly," Taliya said, not sure exactly what this human knew about why the surveillance was being established.

"We'll be spacing them about every fifty yards along the border with the national park. Do the tigran consider it their territory all the way to here?"

"The clan leader tells me they rarely come this far west, but yes, they consider it their territory."

The man nodded and stooped to pick up a camera before heading to the first tree. Taliya watched as he used sharp points on the tips of his boots to kick into the trunk and work his way up about twenty feet to disguise the camera among the branches but still have a clear view of the ground below.

The other technician approached more cautiously. *She must not have much experience with tigran*, Taliya decided.

"This will take all day," she said hesitantly. "You don't have to stay with us the whole time."

"Actually, I do," Taliya said. "I have assured not only the tigran living here but the president herself that I will oversee the whole process."

The woman's eyes grew wide, but she nodded and got back to work. Taliya was glad she didn't feel like chatting because the aroma of her presence was enough to make the tigran want to gag and cover her sensitive nose— aggressive human body odor mixed with garlic and onion. Maybe the technician didn't see the point of bathing before climbing around in the woods for hours.

Throughout the day, the technicians climbed and hung small cameras while Taliya watched from the sidelines. For lunch, she munched on some dried venison the clan had provided. The workers grabbed quick nutrition bars but did not take a break. They probably wanted to be sure they were long gone before darkness set in around them—not to mention dozens of wild tigran. For bathroom breaks, they always headed onto the ranchers' side, never toward where creatures might be lurking.

Occasionally, she'd notice the techs glancing off into the forest, and she wondered if they'd spotted one of the two male tigran. Kano would have to hide himself carefully. White fur did not camouflage in the fall trees. She didn't know if it really mattered whether the workers figured out she wasn't the only one watching, but she definitely knew Severo didn't want to meet the humans. He wasn't thrilled about their presence in the first place.

Finally, after rigging miles of trees, the technicians started packing up their cart.

"That should do it," the male tech said. "We ended right here at the Ute Reservation line. Our company will monitor the feed and forward you any images that are captured."

"Thank you," Taliya said.

He nodded and extended his hand, which she shook, then both technicians climbed in the cart and headed off slowly through the forest. The rustling of leaves and snaps of branches behind her indicated one of the male tigran was following the humans. Severo emerged from the trees and joined her.

"Kano says he will watch until they are well clear of our land," he said.

Taliya nodded. That she'd heard any noise should have told her it wasn't Severo following the techs. He moved through the forest nearly soundlessly.

The clan leader headed to the nearest rigged tree and looked up at the camera, then he froze and did a weird head tilt, his mouth open. When he turned back to Taliya, it took every fiber of her civilized being not to burst out laughing. His nose wrinkled, whiskers flared, and his bristly tongue stuck all the way out of his fanged mouth. Massive, imposing Severo was making the most dramatic "stinky face" she'd ever seen—though she'd never seen another tigran do that at all. When he finally stopped, he shook his head, maybe to clear his nose.

"One of those humans needs a grooming."

Taliya chuckled because he wasn't wrong, but it did make her wonder more about the differences between the groups of tigran. This clan had spiked tongues and whatever that organ was called on the roof of their mouths that led to the stinky face. There seemed to be actual genetic variances between the tigran choosing to live wild from those who lived among humans. Scientists would love to investigate that more—determine if those variances were what led them to run from human contact—but she knew the clan would have no interest in being studied by a species that had nearly wiped them out of existence.

"That's it, then. Kano has his GSP system thing," Severo said, bringing her back to the moment. "He can find his way to camp."

Taliya nodded and didn't correct him.

He started off, and she followed, embarrassed by how much noise she made along the way.

⸺◈⸺

Curled in their bed of leaves covered by a deer hide, Taliya whispered to Kano about Severo's reaction to the smelly technician. Kano muffled his laughter. Tigran had excellent hearing. Taliya rested her head on his chest and wrapped her tail around his leg. Kano cuddled her in under his arm. It was cold enough after dark that they both slept fully dressed.

"I have never, ever, seen a tigran do that," he whispered back. "I'd pay serious money to see Severo make stinky face."

"I'm not sure he realizes that's odd for tigran to do. I'd

always thought the uncivilized tigran had made a choice to live separately, but maybe there's much more to it, right at the genetic level. We're all still experiments. Who knows what variations there were along the way?"

"Within any species," he whispered, "there are unique temperaments among the creatures. I always assumed it was just a resistance to living so properly. The government scientists would love to hear your theory."

"Not a chance. If we have any hope of getting the clan this land and some independence, they need to be as uninteresting to humans as possible."

Kano gave her shoulder a squeeze in agreement.

The whole adventure so far had been fascinating, but Taliya hesitated to share any of it, even with the president. This clan of wild tigran had been through so much devastation. The last thing they needed was humans wanting to study and investigate them. Her only goal was to resolve the dispute with the ranchers and help come to an agreement about official land boundaries. Then Severo's clan could live in peace. Hopefully.

The tigran still up and moving around them blended into the woods, but Kano's visible head was like a pile of snow on a full-moon night. A giggling kit broke the silence. Taliya gazed up at the stars peeking through the trees in the clearing where they all slept and missed her own trio of kits.

"I'm sure Marla is doing fine and everything is well," Kano said, as if reading her thoughts. "President Nakobi even sent those extra soldiers to help guard the compound while we're gone. The kits are okay."

"I know, but I still miss them. Maybe we can come visit another time and bring the whole family. Someone will need to check in with the clan from time to time."

"That's an excellent idea," Kano said.

"We'd love that," Jacy answered from nearby.

"Us too," Taliya said back.

Taliya hoped Jacy hadn't overheard the entire conversation, but they had been whispering carefully for the early part. She and Kano curled up tighter together to sleep under the stars on the chilly fall night in the Colorado forest.

THE FIRST IMAGES TALIYA RECEIVED FROM THE SURVEILLANCE system were only raccoons and deer and other wildlife in the area. She shared them with Severo and Jacy and other interested clan members, and the kits were fascinated with how the technology worked. She was confident none of the tigran would be on camera, even if they had been the ones crossing the territory line before. The whole clan knew the system was there. It couldn't necessarily prove their innocence, but it could show if something else was going on.

That information came two days after the cameras were installed. Taliya was learning to appreciate pine nuts when she felt her com buzz in her pocket. Stepping aside from the group to answer, she saw the call was from President Nakobi herself.

"Hello, Padme," Taliya said to her friend.

"Hello, Wild Taliya. How's uncivilized life going?"

Taliya chuckled. "It's rather like that *camping* I've heard so much about."

"Ah, camping. My children love to do that. I'm a bigger fan of a nice warm bed. Anyhow, we have an interesting development. One of the ranchers sent a notice today that several tigran attacked his herd overnight, killing three large cows and dragging them back into their territory in the woods."

"Fascinating," Taliya said, "because I can assure you this group wasn't involved in anything like that."

"I've been told the videos show not a single tigran anywhere near the territory line, let alone dragging hundreds of pounds of dead cow."

"So what happens now?"

"I've sent a small team to the ranch to investigate. I'm curious to see if the owner can provide proof of this attack. Obviously, we will not indicate that we doubt him, merely that we are gathering evidence. What he describes would leave some gory mess behind."

"I would think so," Taliya agreed.

"I'll update you once I know more."

"Thanks, Madame President. Talk to you soon."

Taliya disconnected the call and turned to find Jacy watching her intently.

"Another attack has been reported by a local rancher," Taliya said. "A team is being sent to investigate."

"But the camera things will show we did not cross that line," Jacy said.

"Yes, it's clear proof something else is going on."

Jacy nodded and returned to gathering pine cones. Taliya joined in, but her mind wasn't on the task. What would the investigators find? Were the ranchers lying, or was some animal violently attacking their herds? A mountain lion or a bear wouldn't take down three cows and drag them away.

She was there to get answers and resolve this conflict, and she hoped that resolution would come sooner rather than later. Even after a few days, she missed Amrita, Little Jai, and Aliania. Maybe she could video chat with them before bed tonight. The kits would love a chance to meet some creatures like them who lived so differently.

Later that afternoon, Taliya's com received an image from one of the cameras: two wildlife agents in official-looking uniforms standing at the property line—one male and one female. The next image showed them waving at the camera. She realized they wanted her to come meet them. A note quickly followed confirming the coordinates where they were waiting.

Kano was off with Jacy, learning new methods of how to tan a deer hide, so Taliya responded to the note, saying she was on her way, informed Severo that they might have some answers, and set off on her own. Even at a jog, it took about thirty minutes to reach the agents. When she arrived, they greeted her with worried faces.

"Are you Taliya?" the woman asked.

"Yes, I'm your contact."

"I'm Ruth, and this is Ted. We're agents with the Parks and Wildlife Division."

"They sent you to investigate the attack on the ranch," Taliya confirmed.

"Quite violent and nasty," Ruth said. "Literally blood and guts. We found the carcasses about a hundred yards from the scene."

"So you actually found dead cattle? No tigran left the camp last night. They did not do this."

"We have an even more dangerous conclusion."

Ruth passed a white claw sheath to Taliya. It took her a minute to process what it was. Definitely the outside of a claw that had been shed or torn off, but from a much larger and more solid claw than any tigran she'd ever seen.

Taliya flared out her own claws as an example. "It's too big for a tigran."

"We'll have it analyzed," Ted said, "but I already have my suspicions. This is too big for a puma or a bobcat, and it's not from a bear."

"We suspect," Ruth said, "that it came from a full-blooded lion or tiger."

"In the woods *here*?"

"Areas like this are hard to police," Ruth said. "We know there are tigers and lions and other big cats still in private homes, laws or no laws. As you well know, collectors don't much care about any of that."

Taliya flinched, thinking immediately of her own unique kits, constantly under threat from unscrupulous humans. Of Reynaldo, the panthran held captive for so many years.

"Some big cats may have gotten loose from a local collector," Ted added. "Or been released to fend for themselves."

"More than one?" Taliya's hackles spiked up her back.

"Why would one tiger take down three cows?" Ruth said. "We suspect three . . . or more."

Taliya pondered that possibility with ears turned back flat, tail puffed. She glanced around nervously, like a gang of tigers might pop out and attack at any moment. A big cat was as different from her as a human was, but at least she and humans could speak the same language and communicate. Rival predators often killed each other in the wild, to eliminate competition. She had no interest in facing off against a lion or a tiger.

"We have offered to rig wildlife cameras to record the fields of several local ranchers," Ruth said, "without letting them know about the cameras already in place at the border. But I think we can eliminate the element of tigran crossing over. Besides the claw, what we found is not how tigran hunt."

Heading off Taliya's question, Ted added, "We've studied the tigran in these woods far more than they know we have. They hunt like the Ute, using weapons and carrying the whole kill back to camp. The cows we saw today were partially eaten on the spot."

"I can't see tigran doing that," Taliya agreed. "Even these tigran. They live wild, but not that wild."

"So we start the search for the roaming big cats," Ruth said with a sigh.

"Hopefully, we can catch them and relocate them to a sanctuary," Ted said. "With so few left in the world, I'd hate to have to euthanize them."

Taliya shuddered in agreement. "The tigran here might be willing to help. They'll want to protect those cats as much as you and also safely remove them from their territory."

"Let the group know what we've found," Ruth said. "See if they have any ideas on how to trap them or if there have been any sightings they failed to mention to you."

"They would have told me if they'd seen a lion or tiger roaming around, but I'll ask." Taliya lifted the claw sheath to her nose and memorized the scent. "I haven't smelled anything like this in the woods."

"Good," Ted said, taking the claw back from her. "We'll be in touch once we analyze this evidence and the bovine remains left behind."

"So the tigran are cleared to claim their land?" Taliya asked.

"That's way above my pay grade," Ruth said with a sad smile. "You'll have to take that up with the powers that be."

"We'll be in contact with other locals, to warn them,"

Ted said. "And the Ute Reservation Council will be notified. They might also have ideas on how to track the big cats."

Ruth shook Taliya's hand before leaving. "We'll let you know when we have the test results back or any updates. Keep your com handy."

Taliya nodded, and the pair headed toward their small transport. She watched until they were out of sight in the forest.

Walking through the woods alone, Taliya found herself much more aware of every little noise and strange smell. She'd been blasting through the forest fecklessly, considering herself a bigger threat than anything else living there. Now she shifted into a run, less worried about making noise than getting back in one piece.

At camp, she gathered Kano, Severo, and Jacy and let them know what the investigators had found.

"A tiger?" Jacy whuffed. "Like a real *tiger*?"

"Or a lion," Taliya said. "Or a combination of the two. They felt confident there are at least three of them. The wildlife folks will have to run some tests on the evidence before they know for sure, but definitely big cats who don't belong in Colorado."

"We'll post extra guards," Severo said, "to keep an eye on a broader area."

"You have guards posted?" Taliya asked.

With a toothy smile, Jacy said, "How do you think we caught you so far away from our actual camp?"

"We're alert for another random attack," Severo said

with a frown. "If we'd been better prepared a year ago, there would still be several clans in this area."

That pulled the smile from Jacy's face, and Taliya chuffed sadly. Hopefully, the guards could prevent a silent big cat attack. There were vulnerable kits to protect.

Jacy and Severo headed off to meet with their group, and Taliya and Kano sat down on a nearby fallen tree. She pulled out her com and shot off a message to the president. The wildlife agents may have already updated Padme, but Taliya wanted to be sure she was fulfilling her responsibilities as well.

"So are the tigran exonerated?" Kano asked.

"It seems so. I'm not sure if that will make the ranchers happy or not. And now there's dangerous big cats in the mix. The issues over the land still need to be resolved. I'm hoping we'll get the all clear to start documenting what the clan considers their territory so we can make it official and gain protected status as a reservation."

"One step closer, I guess. How about we call and chat with the kits? That will cheer you up."

Without waiting for her response, Kano tapped in a call to their compound from his com.

"Papa! Mama!" the kits all squealed into the phone, crowding the video feed so their parents were mostly looking up their noses.

"My kittens!" Taliya said in response, as they fully expected her to.

CHAPTER 3

While the wildlife officers conducted their tests, Taliya was given the go-ahead to begin plotting the area the uncivilized tigran considered their land. Using GPS and physically walking the territory—because the clan knew landmarks, not coordinates—they were to determine all of the hoped-for borders. Taliya expected Ruth and Ted were also hoping the tigran found evidence of the wild big cats. She hoped they discovered clues but no actual tiger or lion. There was no way an encounter like that would end well. It would break her heart to have to kill one of the few remaining tigers in the world, even to save herself.

The land where Severo's clan lived was technically part of San Juan National Forest, but employing park service rangers and caring for national lands had fallen by the wayside decades ago. The government had been selling it off, chunk by chunk, along the borders to ranchers.

Fortunately, the territory in question was a heavily wooded and mountainous section of the park and not practical for cattle. Taliya suspected the ranchers wanting the land had more to do with the constant human desire to own things rather than actual need or usefulness.

Her mapping showed the lake near the tigran camp was actually the Vallecito Reservoir. It was a glorious, beautiful area. In the bit of research she'd done before the trip, Taliya had learned most of the region was once used for camping and tourists. Those sites had been closed down over the decades, though she suspected some brave humans still snuck in to hike and climb the tallest mountains.

When she'd asked about this, Jacy admitted they did spot humans now and then. As long as the trespassers didn't appear threatening, the clan left them to their own devices. And no, the tigran hadn't killed a single soldier during the war. They had been hiding and avoiding human contact at all costs. Soldiers disappearing was either propaganda nonsense or due to something else.

Possibly stray tigers or lions.

It made Taliya wonder how long the cats had been loose in the mountains and where they'd come from. Maybe it had just taken them time to discover the smorgasbord of cows on the ranch lands.

To the south, the Nuche and the tigran had agreed to a border between their lands generations ago, and Taliya expected the government would honor that. Another simple border was on the west between what the tigran considered their territory and the edge of the ranchers' lands—where the surveillance system had been installed—at the edge of the mountain range outside Durango. Severo walked that land with Taliya again and confirmed those borders. It got a bit dicey because the city of Montrose had to be avoided. He agreed to an invisible line straight up from Highway 550.

Severo admitted the tigran often traveled as far east as the Monte Vista Wildlife Refuge, but they never strayed or hunted within its borders. He understood they couldn't claim all of the land, so that would be the direction to discuss first. It included the Rio Grande National Forest, and the government had power over how that area was used. Highway 160 was a good place to end the eastern side. The horrific influenza outbreak of 2078 had killed off a third of the residents of Colorado, but a few dozen folks still lived in South Fork. How would they feel about suddenly being part of a tigran reservation?

North was also a concern. There were no large cities in that area, and Severo said they often traveled up to the Gunnison River, though they stayed clear of what was left of the nearby town. As small as the clan was now, it would be hard to justify thousands of acres for the reservation, but their numbers would restore over time. She had to keep her eye on the future and pull all the government "restitution" strings she could to ensure them a territory large enough for generations to come. She set her sights on land up to Gunnison for the northern border.

When they'd arrived, Taliya and Kano had come in

from the east and left their transport just outside Pagosa Springs, where it would be easily reachable if they needed it. Heading that way first, they could get a change of clothes and give their devices a charge from the main solar source in the truck. So, they decided to hike to the east with Severo, to determine how far on that side was necessary to claim for his group, then turn north. Two large males—under Jacy's direction—would be left in charge of keeping the clan safe from whatever hungry felines were roaming the forest.

The trio set out at first light two days later and were making good time, though the routes Severo chose were not the mostly flat trails Taliya and Kano had used on their trip in.

"It's not like you can't stray outside the determined borders," Taliya said as they hiked and she noted coordinates on the GPS, "but the land we claim would be protected for your use. Humans wouldn't be allowed to hunt or build inside of your reservation."

"Being so close to the wildlife refuge may be a benefit," Kano added as he stopped to catch his breath along the mountain pass. "Those areas are already restricted."

Severo paused and waited for him, though Taliya thought he looked amused by the effort hiking up mountains required of the two civilized tigran. Taliya's family had always lived simply in the forest—closer to how the clan lived than the technology-obsessed human world—but neither she nor Kano had ever dealt with hiking true mountains. It was definitely rough on the thighs. And she was now very clear on how much less oxygen there was up so high. While they were stopped, Taliya scrolled around on the satellite images of the area.

"Even though there's not much population in Pagosa Springs, I know your territory won't be able to encompass that. Highway 160 can work as a border there, all along the southeast, but staying clear of the city itself. The area widens out as you go more northeast toward other towns."

Severo appeared to consider that, using whatever images he held in his mind as reference points. The GPS was interesting to him but didn't work as well for the wild tigran as his own internal compass.

"It's a full-day hike from home. And despite the tempting hot springs there, we never enter the city area. Too many humans. But do you think we can get that much land to the east?"

"All these mountains make it ridiculous to claim for farming or cattle," Taliya said. "It should be acceptable, as long as you agree to a few campers and climbers."

"We don't mind the humans who keep to their own business. Adventurous hikers are usually respectful of the land and everything living there."

Kano nodded his agreement and then started out again along the steep trail. The other two followed him. Taliya could see from the coordinates that they were still many miles from their transport. It would take them all day to reach it. Taliya and Kano couldn't maintain their normal roughly four-mile-an-hour gait on the rough terrain. The trio would spend the night camping near Pagosa Springs before heading northeast along what was hopefully the new tigran reservation border.

The biggest challenge ahead was the over one hundred miles up to the Gunnison River to explore the northern border. She hated to admit that actually walking that far seemed impossible. It might be necessary, but she hoped they could avoid it. On the map, she could see the obvious square-like area the reservation could encompass.

The section of land she wanted for the tigran was significantly larger than the Ute Reservation. Would that be a problem? The tigran needed to hunt, while the Nuche didn't rely that heavily on hunting for their food, and they were connected with bigger reservations to the south. An expansive portion of land for the wild tigrans' future was vital. Severo would certainly want to nail down as much land as he could. It was his duty to fight for his clan and the generations to come. She would have to battle alongside him as best she could.

They arrived at the transport before dark, and Taliya and Kano plugged in their communicators to charge. While Severo scoped out the area for a good spot to sleep, she wondered if he would be offended if she spent the night in the transport. Or pulled out the tent and camping equipment they'd brought but decided not to lug along with them. Sleeping under the stars was a unique experience. Having things drop out of trees on her in the middle of the night was something she wouldn't mind avoiding. Ticks were bad enough in Arkansas, but she'd lost count of how many she and Kano had pulled from their fur after days of sleeping in piles of leaves.

As she pondered this, her communicator dinged with a message from the wildlife division stating the claw sheath they'd found did indeed belong to a tiger. The genetics were mixed from several species, so it was a privately kept animal, not one from a zoo that would preserve the purity of the different species for conservation efforts. They had also found fur from a male lion on one of the dead cows.

So at least one tiger and one lion. Probably more.

While her original mission seemed to be on track, Taliya suspected she and Kano were not heading home until those animals were found. They couldn't just leave dangerous big cats roaming around. Their next victim might be human or tigran instead of bovine.

———⊹⊱◈⊰⊹———

AFTER A LONG NIGHT WHERE THEY TOOK TURNS STAYING AWAKE and on guard—and Taliya and Kano enjoyed the comfort of pillows in the back of the transport—the trio headed northeast to confirm that boundary. Taliya's muscles hadn't ached so badly since her torturous run-in with a cattle prod when she was kidnapped from the refugee camp. From the way Kano was moving, he felt the same. Severo just plowed ahead. She smiled at the realization he'd probably made journeys like this with a dead buck swung over his shoulder.

Before they'd stopped for lunch, Severo began to slow down and pay more attention to the forest around them. While Taliya was grateful for a bit of a break, it also unnerved her. What was he sensing? He paused and smelled the air with his mouth open. A serious stinky face followed, but this time it wasn't funny at all.

"What is it?" she asked.

"A fresh kill, not far away. And scents I don't recognize."

"The big cats?" Kano asked with a frown.

"It seems too far away from where the cows were killed," Severo said, "but maybe all the humans investigating scared them off and made them aim for new hunting grounds. They've had a few days to travel."

"We should check it out." Taliya pulled the communicator from her pocket. "I wonder if they showed up on the surveillance system. Not sure that's being monitored consistently anymore. I'll get some pictures. Maybe there'll be tracks so we can tell where they're heading. You don't think they're still around, do you?"

Severo shook his head. "The unfamiliar smells are lingering, not active."

They headed into the trees, following the scent of blood and on high alert. The three of them might not be the only ones looking for the kill. Wolves, bears, or mountain lions, who do belong in the Colorado wilds, should be avoided too.

"There," Kano said, pointing to their right.

They approached cautiously, but the area seemed to be clear of predators. The kill itself—a deer—was nearly picked clean. The smell of it was still quite fresh. Vultures were circling overhead. If they hadn't landed yet, the site hadn't been unoccupied for long.

"Look here," Severo said, bending down to investigate several large paw prints. "These are too big to be a puma. And the variety of sizes shows three or four different cats."

Taliya snapped photos of the prints, the kill, and the area around them. She could smell evidence of both a tiger and a lion—she'd seen one in a zoo once. Noting their exact location on the GPS, she sent it all to Ted in the Wildlife Division. He responded quickly.

> Agree that it looks like tiger prints. Be careful! We will send a team from Monte Vista Wildlife Refuge to investigate. They have trucks in that area doing research.

"A team is headed this way from the wildlife refuge," she said. "I hope they bring tranq darts and nets because these animals are not far away."

"After eating this much," Kano said, "they've probably found a spot to sleep."

"We should try to locate them," Severo said, standing and scanning the area. He glanced back at the tracks, then followed them off into the trees.

Taliya and Kano exchanged looks. They were not remotely prepared to deal with wild big cats if they found them. Hurrying after him so they weren't separated, Taliya chuffed to get his attention. Severo paused and turned back to her.

"What do you plan to do if we find a group of sleeping tigers?" she asked.

"Share the location through your thing there," he said, pointing at her communicator.

"You won't try to engage them?"

Severo frowned at her like she'd talked about magic fairies. "Of course not."

"Good," Taliya said, motioning for him to continue following the tracks.

A few minutes later, they all paused at the distant sound of a motorized vehicle.

"Guess the team has arrived," Taliya said.

The wind shifted, and the smell of tiger wafted over them. The animals were close.

Severo chuffed quietly, though Taliya sensed it was meant for the wild tigers—one bit of communication they could share. She chuffed as well. Kano turned in a circle, tracing the scent. When he stopped, Severo was facing the same way. Taliya nodded her agreement. The tigers—and lions as well—were not far off to their left.

Severo moved silently in that direction. Taliya stayed put and reached out a hand to keep Kano with her. They tended to sound like wounded animals in the woods, snapping twigs and making what Jacy liked to call an "alarming amount of noise." Rather like most bumbling humans. Severo returned, nodding his head.

"They are asleep," he whispered. "Two tigers and two lions, a male and female of each."

"Great gods." Taliya glanced past him into the trees.

Kano and Severo looked at her expectantly, and it took her a second to register what they were waiting for. She pulled up the GPS again and sent Ted their coordinates with the new information.

> Keep an eye on them. We are gathering a
> team that can assist in a capture. Hold
> tight! If they wake up, get out of
> their way.

She showed the response to the males, and they nodded agreement. Taliya carefully stepped over to sit on a fallen log. They might be there for a while. Kano and Severo seemed less willing to settle in.

"I'm going back to keep an eye on them," Severo said, "like he recommended. If they start to wake up, I'll clear out."

It seemed risky, but Taliya knew being surprised by a tiger in the woods was an even bigger risk. She nodded, and the wild tigran soundlessly slipped into the forest.

"How does he do that?" Kano whispered. "So big, but so silent."

"A lot of practice."

A grumbling growl came from the woods. Severo. Probably telling them to be quiet.

CHAPTER 4

It was close to an hour before they heard whispered bits of conversations and lots of clunking noises heading toward them. She started to appreciate how loud she and Kano seemed to the clan of wild tigran. Those humans hundreds of yards away could easily wake the sleeping big cats.

Taliya stood and joined Kano, who hadn't managed to sit during the entire wait, too much adrenaline flooding through him. It wasn't clear if they would be asked to help, but she would do everything in her power to make sure the big cats were secured without anyone being hurt on either side. Shooting the cats would be easy. What police might resort to. She hoped the team from a wildlife conservation area would be more respectful. There were plenty of safe homes in sanctuaries for the cats once they were secured, even one near their compound in Arkansas.

Severo appeared from the trees. "They are stirring," he whispered. "Hopefully they don't really wake before the rescue team arrives." He sniffed the air. "Almost here."

A waft of fear rose from the normally placid Severo, and Taliya was reminded of his limited—overwhelmingly violent—experience with unknown humans.

"You can make yourself scarce," Taliya offered, "unless we need you."

"Gods," Kano said. "I hope we don't *need* you for this."

Severo nodded and slipped back into the trees, this time farther away from the waking cats. He left just in time because a whole herd of humans snapped branches and tromped their way through the woods toward them. Taliya was amazed Ted had managed to gather such a large group so quickly. And they looked well-prepared. Some carried huge stretchers. Some lugged thick rope nets. One had a pile of bath towels. Most of them had rifles but also what she recognized as tranquilizer dart guns. Her heart raced, remembering more than once when she'd been on the receiving end of a dart. Kano moved closer to her and chuffed reassuringly.

The man who seemed to be the team leader approached the tigran.

"Taliya. Kano," he said with a nod. "I'm Kurt. Are the cats still nearby?"

"Yes," Taliya whispered. "And they surely heard you coming."

The man hunched his shoulders and did that funny

grimace humans use when they know they've screwed up. "We're hoping to dart them quickly and then carry them back to our truck. We have to do this with mountain lions and bears on occasion, when they're too close to human populations or are injured."

"These cats can already smell you and everything you brought with you," Kano said.

Kurt frowned. "So there are four, right? Two tigers and two lions?"

"That's what we've seen," Taliya confirmed, leaving out the fact she hadn't actually seen them herself.

"We'll try to dart all four at the same time, but it takes a bit for the drugs to fully kick in. Everyone needs to stay clear until they're down."

That hadn't been Taliya's personal experience with tranq darts, but it didn't seem like this was Kurt's first rescue so she would trust his lead.

"And those rifles?" Taliya said, glancing at the rest of the team waiting behind him.

"Only a very last resort," Kurt assured her. "And only if lives are in danger. If one of the cats gets away, we'll find it later. This far into the forest, there's no humans to worry about."

Taliya nodded, hoping this was true. She pointed in the direction of the previously sleeping cats.

"They know you're here," she reminded him. "But they don't know exactly what you're up to."

"Understood," Kurt said.

He raised one arm and motioned the team forward. Those with the tranq guns took the lead, and those with rifles followed close behind. The rest stayed back and out of the way. Their job wouldn't begin until the cats were safely sedated. Taliya wrestled with which side she should be on. Kano followed the gun-toting team, so she joined him, though the last thing she wanted was to watch an animal be drugged—or shot and killed. If she could do anything to keep that from happening, she would.

Kurt raised his arm again, but this time with a closed fist. Everyone in the group froze. He motioned directions to the four men with tranq guns, and they spread out. Through the trees up ahead, Taliya could see the distinctive orange of the tigers.

A growl rumbled through the pines and vibrated in her chest. They were definitely awake.

Everything was still for a moment. Even the birds were silent.

Kurt whistled sharply.

It felt like the forest exploded.

The chaos only lasted a few seconds, but for Taliya, the events moved in slow motion and out of focus.

At Kurt's whistle command, the tranq guns were fired —one for each cat. All four leapt up instantly, growling and snarling, thrashing hundreds of pounds of furious claws and muscle through the undergrowth in different directions.

The distinct aroma of terror assaulted her nose, bringing back sharp focus and clarity. Kurt shouted something, but she couldn't make out the words over the roaring, screaming, and crashing confusion. Two of the dart guns fired again, and a man swore. Taliya spotted the team members with rifles moving into place.

"No!" she yelled, rushing toward them.

"Taliya!" Kano called after her. "Get out of there!"

"Watch out!" Kurt yelled.

Taliya used her body to block the closest gun, her back to the shooter. "Just wait," she ordered, arms spread wide.

The lions were hard to see, but the undergrowth shifted as they staggered along, already succumbing to the sedatives. One tiger was nowhere to be seen. What Taliya was confronted with was the second tiger only a few yards away.

Without a single dart stuck in her fur.

The cat's ears were back flat on her head, fur spiked, and she had already begun the growl/hiss rage noise that Taliya understood perfectly. The scent of fear whirled in the air—both from the cats and the humans. Pity for this poor, terrified animal clenched at Taliya's gut. She wished she could talk to the cat and assure her it was all going to be okay. Or at least not painful and horrible.

Taliya and the tiger stared at each other. The sight and smell of her seemed confusing to the cat. She'd probably never been near a tigran before. Taliya chuffed, and the tiger hesitated at the familiar sound. She chuffed again, and the tiger growled.

The pop of a tranq gun sounded, and the tiger jumped and screamed, lashing out in search of what had stabbed her. The cat had been darted, finally, but that didn't mean she was down yet.

In a massive leap, the tiger made a break for it. The men with guns moved out of the way, not comprehending the danger unfolding. They knew the tiger would fall soon. Taliya, however, calculated the direction of the escape and instantly realized the cat was heading straight for the waiting unarmed team members.

Without hesitation, Taliya ran after the tiger, but it had the lead on her and could run much faster. Shouts and yells and the sound of Kano's frantic voice called from behind as Taliya raced after the furious and terrified tiger. Her heart pounded, remembering that feeling so vividly—knowing the drugs would be kicking in and making the animal's brain and logic foggy.

This tiger was even more dangerous now. It was panicking.

Taliya burst into the clearing behind the tiger and assessed the situation in a split second. The cat had stopped and faced the humans, and they were all wide-eyed with shock. Taliya could hear the rest of the team behind her, crashing through the forest, but they wouldn't have a clear shot in time. Anxiety raced through her body as Taliya watched the cat crouch slightly and tense up, her eyes on a target. The imminent attack didn't register on the shocked face of the pretty young blonde holding a stack of towels, but Taliya was already in motion. With a leap, she was on top of the tiger, grabbing her around the neck with both arms.

Pandemonium erupted—the team yelling and screaming and running either toward her or for cover. Taliya hoped they wouldn't shoot if it risked hitting her. All she needed to do was keep the tiger occupied until the drugs took over.

"Wait!" she yelled. "Just wait!"

They were roughly the same size—the stray tiger and Taliya—but only one of them felt like she was fighting for her life. Taliya hung on, using her body weight to keep the tiger from escaping while the big cat snarled and growled and thrashed. With a mighty heave, the tiger rolled on her side, trying to break free, but Taliya wrapped one leg around the tiger's middle to keep her back legs at bay and just clung on tighter. As long as she could keep the claws and fangs away, it could all end well.

The forest had gone quiet except for the screams from the pinned tiger.

Kano growled, "Don't even think about it."

No one was going to shoot in their direction with him around, and he must think she had the tiger under control or he would have jumped in to help.

Taliya chuffed quietly over and over, hoping it would help calm the animal, but the cat's legs continued to thrash and the pitch of her screams grew higher and louder. Finally, the tiger began to relax. Taliya could feel the muscles under her become slack. The screaming stopped, and only feeble growls escaped the tiger's mouth. Taliya relaxed her hold a bit to make sure the cat could breathe well enough, but she didn't let go. Not until she was sure. Death by tiger would only take a split second if she wasn't careful.

When the tiger finally collapsed into drug-induced sleep, one of the men from the team approached. After some quick checks on the cat—scanning a light across her eyes and watching for a reaction—he motioned for the blonde woman with the towels. She approached shakily and wrapped a large bath towel around the cat's face to cover her eyes.

"It helps them to stay asleep if there's no stimulation," she whispered.

Two men with a large stretcher approached, and another team member with a rope net joined them.

"You can let go now, Taliya," Kurt said quietly. "She's asleep. Let's get her in the truck."

Taliya nodded and rolled away from the sedated tiger. Kano was at her side immediately, pulling her up into a painfully tight hug.

"You're crazy," he rumbled into her ear.

Taliya could smell the anxiety radiating from him, even if his words were simple and direct. She laughed nervously and pulled away to catch her breath.

"You saved me," the blonde woman said. She still hovered nearby, clutching the rest of the towels to her chest. Tears streamed down her cheeks.

"I saved both of you."

Thank you, the woman mouthed before she was caught up in the recovery of the other three sedated cats.

"That tiger would have killed you if it could," Kano said, clutching her tightly with one arm.

"I know," she admitted, "but they would've shot her. And she might have mauled that poor human first. I had to do something."

Kano hugged her fiercely again and buried his face in her neck. She wished she could hide the fact she was now shaking as the adrenaline wore off, but her mate simply held her close and kept the rest of his reprimands to himself. For now.

They moved to the side to avoid the frenzy of the wildlife team. It looked like disorder, but watching closely, Taliya noticed the choreographed art of a well-rehearsed dance. Each member knew what they should do, and the whole group played a role. The scariest assignment was the person who had to first approach each sleeping cat and basically poke it with a stick to make sure it didn't react. She wondered how often a seemingly sedated animal turned out to be awake enough. The hackles rose along her neck at that thought.

Within fifteen minutes, all four cats were on stretchers, towels over their faces, secured down with the rope nets, and being carried to the truck—each cat requiring six people to lift the stretcher. Kano offered to help with that bit, but he was assured it was all in hand. Kurt stopped to talk with them before leaving.

"I promise, we will transport them carefully. Thanks

for your help with all of this. We may never know for sure where they came from, but if a few cows are the worst of the victims, we can consider ourselves lucky. If one of them had killed a human . . ."

"They'd be shot," Taliya concluded without emotion.

Kurt shrugged. "It would have been out of our hands."

"Thank you for seeing them safely to new homes," she said. "I'll check with Ted later and find out where they end up."

"It may take a while. We'll do vet checks and learn what we can about them first. If the lions have clean genetics, they may be able to join a zoo and conservation efforts. The tigers are probably too mixed genetically. We'll find a refuge for them."

"Thank you," Kano said. "We're glad we could help save them."

With a nod, Kurt followed the big cats and the rest of the team along the trail to their trucks. Taliya and Kano watched until the last member was long out of sight. She smelled Severo join them before she heard or saw him.

"That was more excitement than I had expected from this day," he said with a fang-filled smile.

"To say the least," Kano added.

Severo motioned at Taliya's clothing. "You look a bit wild yourself now."

She glanced down and laughed. Every inch of her front was covered with tiger fur. She shook and brushed off what she could, but the rest was staying put. The smell of the fur mingled with her tigran scent in an interesting blend.

"So much power," she said. "That dart must have already kicked in, or I wouldn't have been able to hold her."

Kano moaned at the thought, and she gave him a quick hug.

"What now?" Severo said. "I can't imagine you're up to more hiking today."

"How far are we from a good place to make camp?" Taliya asked.

"I know you wanted to travel all the way to the Gunnison River and confirm the landmarks with me, but there are some significant mountains between us and the river. It's wonderful hunting grounds, but not so great for hiking."

"Do we *really* need to physically see it?" Kano asked Taliya. "It's a pretty obvious territory divider."

While she felt responsible for establishing the reservation boundaries, she wondered if they actually needed to set foot on any of them.

"I suppose not," Taliya agreed, silently expressing gratitude to the universe for sparing her that trek. "And even on this eastern side, we can just go straight up from Highway 160."

"Then I suggest we head to a lake near here for the night," Severo said. "It's a few miles away, but there are old lodges there. It will be enough to keep us dry when the rain hits."

Taliya and Kano both scanned the skies, where a few clouds floated by but there wasn't any sign of rain.

"Trust me," Severo said with a wink. "Storm before dark."

He tapped the side of his nose, and Taliya smiled. If Severo smelled rain, she wouldn't doubt him.

"That lake sounds like a great choice," Kano said, stretching and picking up his backpack. "Lead on, captain."

It was about ten miles to the lake. Not the short hike she'd hoped for, but as Taliya checked her GPS now and then she sighed with gratitude to have avoided the towering mountains just north of them. She'd been ridiculous to think they could explore that far on foot. And it really wasn't necessary. The river was a significant landmark. She didn't need to see it with her own eyes, but maybe she and Kano would drive up there on the highway before heading home, just to be able to say they had.

Severo led them to the Williams Creek Reservoir, which was smaller than the lake area where the tigran lived but just as beautiful. They found the abandoned cabins, and the doors were unlocked—ready for any adventurous travelers in the wilderness who happened by. Kano and Taliya dumped their stuff inside a cabin, and Severo selected one a few spots down from them. Windows were opened to air things out, and Taliya used a broom from the corner to sweep away some dead bugs. Live ones had probably scurried into hiding when the door opened. The cabin was in remarkably good shape for something over a hundred years old. Well-built and, from the smell of it, leak-free.

Then the trio went for a long swim in the lake, Taliya's second skinny-dip of the trip. The cold water soaking into her fur was fantastic after the trying day. She felt a little self-conscious in front of Severo, but he seemed to sense this and averted his eyes when she was out of the lake.

After putting on fresh clothes from her pack, Taliya sent messages to President Nakobi, Ted at the Wildlife Division, and the kits while Kano caught a couple of fish. Severo returned from the woods with two rabbits to fill out dinner. They tidied up a ring of rocks that had been used as a firepit and enjoyed a hearty meal of meat cooked on sticks supplemented with some dried berries from their packs.

Once their bellies were full, the trio stretched out on the beach and relaxed, watching the sun set. The rain hadn't arrived yet, but Taliya could smell it now and feel the change in the air pressure. The temperature was dropping steadily, and she wondered if it might be snow or sleet.

"Taliya," Severo said, "why did you risk your life for that human? I nearly rushed out to stop you when I saw the tiger get ready to spring and you leaping toward it. That was a very rash move. Even if it didn't kill you, it could have left you maimed for life."

"Well, it wasn't just about the woman. I mean, I realized the tiger was going to attack her, mainly because she was in the way. That poor cat was out of her mind with the start of the drugs and all the humans." Taliya hesitated. "I've been drugged like that. More than once. It's an awful, helpless feeling."

Severo eyed her curiously but didn't ask her to elaborate.

"The cat probably thought she'd escaped all that when they broke away from whoever had them held captive," Taliya said. "I was worried about what the men with guns would do. If the tiger attacked the woman, they would've shot it."

"So you were protecting the tiger, not the human?"

"Maybe. A little of both, I suppose. I just needed everyone to come out of the encounter alive."

"*You* seemed to be the one in the greatest danger," Kano grumbled. "What in the world would I have told the kits if you'd been killed by a tiger?"

"It was a split-second decision," she admitted. "I didn't really think of it as risking my life. I just wanted to stop the cat before things spiraled out of control."

"All's well that ends well, I suppose," Kano said. "But maybe try not to jump on any more wild animals during this trip. Or ever."

"I'll try," Taliya said with a laugh.

They watched the sky quietly for a bit longer, then the first few drops of rain started and they headed into the cabins. Taliya was a bit surprised Severo chose to sleep indoors. He must be expecting torrential rain.

It was cozy inside the small cabin, so Taliya and Kano stripped down to enjoy sleeping out of their clothes. The twin wooden beds on hand were not really large enough for a tigran—and didn't provide a mattress anyhow—so they pulled out their sleeping rolls and made a comfy spot on the floor. Soon the wind howled and the rain battered the windows, but the pair of tired tigran settled down for a reasonably comfortable night of sleep.

Kano pulled his wife close to spoon and nuzzled into the fur of her neck.

"You smell like the lake," he whispered. "A little wild and earthy."

"Is that good or bad?"

"Very, very good."

Taliya felt the familiar shift in his body that indicated he was interested in more than just a cuddle. The storm raging outside added an extra sense of privacy, even from Severo's ears. She chuffed and rolled over to face him.

"It will be a while before we're alone again," she said. "We still have another week here, at least."

"Let's hope for an uneventful conclusion to the trip."

"You don't want to go hunting for any more big cats in the wilderness?"

He moaned and pulled her close, pressing his forehead against hers and wrapping his tail around her legs. "I knew that tiger was going to kill you. I just knew it."

"I'm sorry," she whispered into his chest.

"When I saw you jump, I knew that was it. That tiger was going to rip you apart. It would have been over before I could help. Can we be done with times I think you're going to die?"

"I hope so. But the last few years of our lives would suggest otherwise."

With a sigh, he kissed her. "Then we should make the most of the time we have."

An hour later, after they had definitely made the most of it, Taliya tried to remember when she was due for her birth control shot, but the date eluded her. She'd have to schedule that as soon as they got home.

CHAPTER 5

The hike back to camp took most of the next day, but it was uneventful. The clan welcomed them and held a bonfire on the lakeshore to celebrate and hear the tale about capturing the tigers and lions. Severo acted out a detailed account of Taliya's wrangling with the tiger, complete with hauntingly accurate snarls and screams that made her tail puff. It seemed like the wild tigran now viewed her with a new respect—more than just some governmental agent.

Once the meal and the stories were done, the clan wandered off to bed. Taliya and Kano stayed by the fire a bit longer with Jacy and Severo.

"So, have we agreed on the borders?" Jacy asked. "At least what we hope to set as boundaries?"

"I think so," Taliya said. "Are you satisfied with what we laid out?"

"Yes." Severo leaned his elbows on his knees. "We

always knew the day would come when humans might want the land we're on. I never expected to have it protected for us."

"If all goes as we hope," Kano said, "the reservation should give you rights over what happens on this land. *Your* land."

"So does that mean you'll be leaving us?" Jacy asked.

"Soon. But not quite yet," Taliya said, "if that's okay."

Jacy tipped her head. "You are welcome for as long as you like."

"I've sent all the details of the proposed reservation to the president. The rest of it is out of my hands. I may be asked to speak to Congress. To help persuade them. But most of what goes on in Washington confuses me. We can just go forward and hope for the best."

"You'll have to return for a visit to let us know," Jacy said with a smile. "So we will meet at least one more time in this life."

"True," Taliya said, returning the smile.

"And maybe you could come in the spring and bring a tigran friend. A *male* friend or two."

Kano raised one black stripe of an eyebrow at Jacy, and she smiled.

"Since the Gathering attack, our numbers are not only down significantly, but our families are too closely related. We have several females of age who are uncomfortable with the choices available. We don't need a genetics lab to tell us that fresh blood is important for the health of our clan's future."

"So you need breeding-age males?" Kano said with a sly grin.

"Yes," Severo said bluntly. "It is vitally important. They wouldn't have to stay. Just visit. And be productive. Males who are handsome and strong would make our young females especially happy."

Taliya was a bit shocked, but the logic made sense. Like the farmers she'd grown up around, the clan needed a couple of bulls to join for a week or two and get the job done.

"I'm sure that can be arranged," Taliya said. "Tigran are scarce now in the U.S., but we are mostly connected on the interwebs. I'll send out some inquires. You might even find that a few want to stay."

"That would be up to the whole clan," Jacy said, "but we would be willing to consider it."

The four tigran sat quietly for a while as the last embers of the fire glowed and were reflected back by the lake. While she was happy to be heading home soon to her busy life with the kits, Taliya knew she would miss her new friends and the simple life they led in the forest. But she did miss a warm, comfortable bed. Even in the time they'd been there, the nights had turned colder.

As they curled up in a pile of leaves that night, Taliya gazed at the stars and compared their location in the Colorado sky to what she normally saw at home in Arkansas. A longing to cuddle with her kits tugged at her heart.

"We can take tomorrow for a bit of a rest," Kano said.

Taliya nodded and snuggled into his chest. "Techs will be here in a day or two, so we can confirm they have removed all of the wildlife cameras. Then we can start the battle with Congress over the reservation. I'm sure a trip to Washington is in my future."

Kano grumbled, as he always did about her plans to be away, and kicked leaves up over their legs. Even with their fur and being fully dressed, it was chilly.

"What happened to that deer hide we were using?" he said. "It wandered off while we were gone."

"Maybe we should pull out the sleeping rolls. The temperature is definitely dropping. I think the clan is ready to move to the caves, but they're waiting for us to leave."

"I'm glad we could help with their winter preparations."

"The kits will love learning all our new skills. Do you suppose they'll like pine nuts? We certainly have an abundance of them around the compound."

"Probably not."

"Maybe we can bring the kits for a visit in the spring. Grandpa Jai might love to come experience real rustic life. Like one of those *vacations* I hear about all the time."

"Good idea," Kano said. "We deserve a real break. I'll hide your communicator so the president can't send you off on a new task."

Taliya snorted and then laughed. There were benefits to being separate from technology now and then.

The sounds of the camp around them grew quiet, but

Taliya found it hard to fall asleep. Snowflakes fluttered in the air. It was only light flurries, but more would be on the way any day now. The flakes disappeared into Kano's white fur.

She smiled at the thought of a soft, warm bed and the hubbub of home.

⸺ ⸙ ⸺

On February 19th, 2177, Congress approved the Tigran Conservation Reservation, including all of the land Taliya and Severo had hoped for.

THE TIGRAN
CHRONICLES:
THE RESCUES
M.W. DENDLER

AT THE CORNER
-OF-
Magnetic
and Main
Meg Welch Dendler
#1 BEST-SELLING, AWARD-WINNING AUTHOR

ABOUT THE AUTHOR

Meg Welch Dendler has considered herself a writer since she won a picture book contest in fifth grade and entertained her classmates with ongoing sequels for the rest of the year. Beginning serious work as a freelancer in the 1990s while teaching elementary and middle school, Meg has more than one hundred articles in print, including interviews with Kirk Douglas, Sylvester Stallone, and Dwayne "The Rock" Johnson. She has won contests with her short stories and poetry, along with multiple awards for her best-selling "Cats in the Mirror" alien rescue cat children's book series. *Bianca: The Brave Frail and Delicate Princess* was named Best Juvenile Book of 2018 by the Oklahoma Writers' Federation, and *Snickerdoodle's Shenanigans* earned the same honor in 2024.

Visit her at www.megdendler.com for more information about upcoming books and events and all of Meg's social media links.

9 798990 827745